Editors: Happily Editing Anns

Cover Design: Cadence Keys

Discreet Cover Design: Lily Bear Design Co.

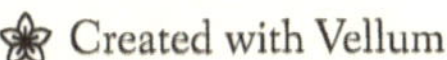 Created with Vellum

ABOUT LAST NIGHT

BREAKING THE RULES
BOOK 3

CADENCE KEYS

To my girlies who love a dirty talking bodyguard who's willing to break all the rules

Rule #1

DON'T TAKE YOUR SAFETY FOR GRANTED

Brynn

Are you fucking kidding me?

If I could punch my asshole ex through the phone, I one thousand percent would.

"Oh no, he did not," my hairstylist, Joy, said as she peered over my shoulder at the phone in my hand showing the latest entertainment news snippet about how my ex was torn up over our breakup. The same breakup that happened over three months ago because I caught him having sex with his massage therapist.

And then that prick had the actual audacity to shout that it was just a "happy ending" like it was normal.

We'd only dated for six months, and I was more embarrassed than upset, but then he had to go and act all heartbroken for the media and paint me as the villain.

And I had to sit here and take it because if a woman stood up for herself—especially a woman as famous as I am—then she'd be labeled an attention-seeking bitch and painted as the villain anyway.

I had too much to do to get ready for this upcoming tour, and I couldn't waste time worrying about this. The press would say whatever they were going to say. I'd learned that lesson a long time ago. It didn't matter what the truth was. It mattered what would help them go viral on social media and get comments.

Unfortunately, tearing women down seemed to be the most effective tool to meet that goal.

Sometimes the state of society was really depressing. I closed the social media app I'd been mindlessly scrolling while Joy worked her magic and stared at myself in the mirror.

On the outside, I'd managed to maintain my polished look despite the increasing feelings of loneliness and exhaustion. I was tired of the grind. I was tired of being torn down for being successful. I was tired of not knowing if the men I dated actually gave a shit about me or were just using me for my fame so they could try to catapult themselves off my hard work.

I was too young to feel this jaded.

I was only twenty-five, but I'd been in this business since I was fifteen. I'd seen and experienced more than most people twice my age. The burden of fame that hung around my neck sometimes—more often lately—made me feel ancient.

Joy finished styling my hair and placed her delicate fingers on my shoulders. "What do you think?"

I smiled up at her, pleased that it actually reached my eyes this time. "You're the best in the biz for a reason. I love it. Thank you, Joy."

She was a gem I'd found by accident and now used her exclusively for all styling and haircuts. I'd wanted to try a new style for the tour and came straight to her. I loved the way the cut framed my face, but I was glad she was coming with me on tour because there'd be no way I could duplicate the actual styling without her.

In another life, I was probably a plain Jane since I never would've looked half as put together as I did with the makeup and hair stylists on my payroll.

I paid her usual rate, but tipped her extra because I never wanted to lose her. She left out the front door, and I watched her drive out until she rounded the bend that led to the front gate. The house itself was hidden from prying eyes by elaborate and beautiful trees and shrubs that I'd hired a whole gardening crew to maintain.

But the privacy was all an illusion. I watched on the security feeds that streamed to my phone as she was faced with at least a dozen paparazzi and their obnoxious cameras.

Switching out of the security app, I called my manager, Stella.

"Almost there! There was a bad accident that shut down half the freeway."

"That's okay. I was just calling to let you know there's a crowd at the gate. Just wanted you to be forewarned."

She let out a low growl that had a small smile tugging at my lips. "I swear to God, I could wring that sleazy little bastard's neck for what he's putting you through. This is ridiculous, Brynn. You don't deserve their harassment."

I shrugged even though she couldn't see me. "They'd harass me regardless. Him whining to the press, trying to make me out to be the bad guy, has just given them a more exciting reason to harass me."

I swore I could hear her frown over the phone. "This isn't okay, Brynn."

"It is what it is."

What else could I say? This came with the territory of being one of the biggest celebrities in the world. If I could change it, I would. I often wondered if they ever thought about what life would be like if the roles were reversed. If celebs started coming to their houses and camping out so they could snag a quick pic and spin it into something salacious.

My phone buzzed with a text, and I pulled it away from my ear to see it was the gate guard telling me a package had just been delivered.

"Can you grab the package that was just delivered at the front gate on your way in?" I asked Stella.

"Sure thing. I'm about five minutes away."

"Okay, see you soon."

I ended the call and then walked out to my back patio. I lived a luxurious life. No one would have any clue how empty it sometimes felt. I stared at the crystalline blue water in my pool and watched the water ripple from the cool breeze. It was soothing in a way, and I got lost in watching the gentle movement until I felt my phone buzz in my hand.

I lifted it up and frowned when I saw a text from an unknown number.

I heard my front door open right as I opened the text, and all the blood drained from my face.

"Brynn!" Stella shouted, and the panic in her tone broke me out of my shock.

I spun around to face her, and her face looked as pale as I imagined mine did. She held a box in her hand that was open.

"There was no sender address, and the gate guard said with all the chaos with the paps he didn't see who actually dropped it off. I thought that was strange, but then it started ringing and the guard opened it to make sure it wasn't a bomb or something."

She held the box out to me and I set my phone face down on the patio table. I took the box from her and set it down. There was a piece of plain white paper open on the top that had clearly caused Stella's concern. The message was typed: ***I'M COMING FOR YOU***. A cheap phone was beneath it, and it was already open displaying the text message and photo I'd just seen on my own phone.

UNKNOWN

YOU'RE A STUPID SLUT WHO DESERVES EVERYTHING COMING TO YOU.

The picture was of a very well done deepfake video of me bleeding to death.

"Brynn, we need to hire better security. This psycho was at the gate!"

I stared at the video playing on repeat. It was short, probably only five seconds, but it played on a loop. I'd had stalkers before—no one got to my level of fame without them—but never this deranged.

Never this violent.

Stella was talking, but I couldn't hear her over the whooshing in my ears as I stared down at the too realistic video of my death.

I'd kept my composure while my name was being dragged through the mud by my ex and through all the times people had come at me because of my success.

But this...

This was too much.

For the first time in a long time, I felt fear for my safety and wondered if this life—the music, the fame, the constant scrutiny—was worth it.

Rule #2

DON'T JUDGE YOUR CLIENT'S BEHAVIOR

Wyatt

My job required me to be attentive at all times, but I sure as shit didn't sign up to listen to the client join the mile high club with a flight attendant.

"Fuck yeah, feel this big dick."

A moan that would make a porn star proud broke through the otherwise silent jet, and I fought the urge to roll my eyes.

I really needed to get Raf to transfer me to a different assignment.

Normally I could ignore the inappropriate behavior of the clients and focus on doing my job with my usual stoic reserve. Lately, though, I'd had a harder time keeping a neutral expression. Maybe it was this particular client—he never listened to any of my safety briefs, talked down to women, and didn't tip his servers.

And that was just the tip of the iceberg.

I scanned the cabin of the plane, but his secretary was enjoying her reprieve from his sexual advances, and the other flight attendant was trying a little too hard to pretend like she had no idea what her counterpart was doing in the bathroom.

I pulled out my phone and shot off a message to my boss and friend, Rafferty Carmichael—the owner of Carmichael Security.

ME

If any new opportunities come in, I call dibs. I can't stand this guy for much longer.

RAF

That bad? You're one of my most patient guys. Should I drop him as a client?

I appreciated that Raf valued my opinion enough to even ask, knowing his business and reputation were on the line. I'd kept thorough notes in my daily logs to him about the client's activities and behavior.

ME

That's your call. You're the boss for a reason.

And he was a damn good one, so I knew he'd do me a solid and reassign me when something new came up.

As I heard my client let out a loud grunt, I sent a silent prayer that Raf would come through soon.

The first thing I did when I walked into my house was open the windows. It had been two weeks since I'd been home, and I hated the stale smell that hung in the air from my house being closed up.

I didn't mind the travel—I'd been moving around for my

jobs since I joined the navy and then the Seals. It was the emptiness that I was forced to come home to that always got me. It's probably why I used to spend so much of my off time with my brother, but that changed once he married his daughter's best friend, Sadie.

I was happy he was happy, but it got a little hard to watch sometimes. My brother deserved the love of a good woman after what his ex-wife had put him through, but it was another reminder of how my life had turned out much different than I'd expected.

Not to mention walking in on them fucking was not high on my wish list, and it had already happened twice. Those two were lucky they weren't rabbits or their house would've been overrun with kids.

I moved to the fridge that only had one bottle of my favorite IPA and a half-full jar of pickles. It wasn't that late, and I could probably run to the grocery store if I could've mustered up the energy.

As it was, I used the edge of the counter to help me pop off my beer top and then slouched on the couch and flipped through the channels. I didn't have cable—I wasn't home enough for it to be worth the cost—but I did have one of the popular streaming services.

I pulled up a documentary on some cult and took a long pull of my beer. I made it through one episode and was just starting the second when my phone started vibrating on my coffee table with an incoming call. I answered as soon as I saw Raf's name on the display.

"Hey, what's up?"

"I've got a new assignment for you."

I sat up and set my beer down on the coffee table. "Who?"

"I'd rather not say over the phone. Can you come in to the office first thing tomorrow morning?"

He was a paranoid bastard, but that's why he was the best at what he did.

"Yeah, I'll be there at eight."

"See you then."

He hung up without any other details, and I grabbed my beer and sat back against my couch, wondering who my new client would be. As long as it wasn't anyone like the dick I'd just been assigned to, I was down.

Raf greeted me as I walked into the main offices for Carmichael Security. The office was a two-story building with the original brick façade from the 1920s, although everything had been remodeled or cleaned up to make it sturdier than it had been when Raf bought it. It was polished, old-fashioned, and unassuming—a lot like the owner.

But once you stepped inside, everything was modern technology, and there were five floors beneath the building —although the blueprints only showed four.

The main floor and second floor were used for meeting with clients, while the bottom floors were where training happened and anything else that Raf didn't want prying eyes on. He had an office both above ground and below, but I knew he only used the one upstairs for show for clients.

Sometimes I thought he felt more comfortable in the dark of the basement offices.

He extended his hand for me to shake, and after I did so, he handed me a folder. "Let's talk more in my office."

He headed to the elevator and pressed the down button.

The ride down to his primary office was short, and I was surprised by the clutter on his desk. "What's all this?"

Normally he kept everything pristine and organized. He waved it away. "A project I'm working on."

I didn't ask more. I'd learned over the years when Raf wasn't ready to talk, he became a vault, and it wasn't worth the time or effort to try to pry him open because he wouldn't share until he was good and ready.

I sat down in the chair across from his and opened the folder. Inside was a picture of a pop star I'd seen on magazines at the store. I'd never listened to her music, but it seemed like she was doing well for herself. Clearly she was doing even better than I'd given her credit for if she could afford Raf.

"Brynn Davis," I said, reading the name at the top of the file.

"She's got a stalker." He flipped the tablet on his desk around and pressed play on a video that seemed to run on a loop. "She was sent a phone with this video on it. It was dropped off at her house, but the gate guard didn't catch who it was. She also got a text to her personal phone that same day." He pointed to the file I was holding, and when I flipped the page, I saw a screenshot of the message. My brow furrowed as I pored over the papers in my hand.

"She doesn't have any additional security besides a gate guard?"

"She has a bodyguard on retainer for when she goes out."

"Who?" I asked, cutting him off from whatever else he was going to say.

"Who do you think?"

There was only one other company in LA at our level, and they were constantly cutting corners. Raf didn't allow any of our clients to only use us for public appearances. There was at least one man on the premises or a very expensive security system and strict protocol if we were hired.

"When do I start?"

"Today too soon?"

The corner of my lips tilted up. "Nope." It's not like I had anything exciting going on at home.

I could only hope Brynn Davis wasn't some shallow pop princess who would drive me up a goddamn wall like so many others had in the past.

This was just another job.

Rule #3

DON'T GET A LADY BONER FOR YOUR NEW BODYGUARD

Brynn

"Is a full-time bodyguard really necessary?" I asked my manager, Stella. I already had such little privacy as it was, the thought of having someone in my space at all hours of the day grated on what little composure I'd managed to maintain since the delivery yesterday.

The worry on her face hadn't gone away for a single second since the box had been delivered, but now there was a hint of relief there as well. "Afraid so. We can't risk your safety, Brynn, and these guys are the best of the best."

I knew she was right—this threat had been worse than any other I'd received in the past—but that didn't make it easier to swallow.

Maybe it was stupid to hate the idea of having a body-guard full-time. I already had them whenever I went out in public; was it really such a big deal to have them with me at all times? Wasn't my safety more important than my privacy? The answer should've been an easy yes, but the truth wasn't that simple.

Stella cleared her throat. "There was another package with a note found last night. It was more graphic than the others and delivered to your private studio."

My studio? That wasn't even in my name. It was under a shell company that was under another shell company because I never wanted to be hounded by press if they found out where it was. We were always careful about when we went and that I was never seen entering or exiting the building.

I felt the blood rush from my face as I unsteadily grasped for the chair behind me. My movements were less than graceful when I sat with a thump.

Stella grabbed my knee and squeezed, and I looked up into her kind brown eyes. "Don't worry, Brynn. We got the best security company money can buy. They're sending over one of their top guys."

I nodded vacantly as I nibbled on my lip and wondered if fame was really worth this. Was it worth looking over my shoulder for the rest of my life? If it wasn't this stalker, would it be someone else? Was I doomed to always be surrounded by people and yet feel so painfully isolated that my heart constantly ached?

A knock sounded on the door, pulling me from my mental spiral. Stella was already halfway there when I stood from my chair. I closed my eyes and took a deep breath while she greeted the person at the door and introduced herself. Her heels clacked on the tile floors of my entryway. Only when I heard her getting closer did I open my eyes and spin around to face her and my new bodyguard.

Every thought in my head evaporated instantly as my gaze slid down the tall, delicious man in front of me. His brown hair looked perfectly styled, and his black suit fit snugly over his broad shoulders, thick biceps, and fit torso. It must've been custom because it didn't fit his frame awkwardly. His face was stern and serious, but his deep brown eyes were observant as he quickly scanned the room before looking at me. His gaze was penetrating, his dark brows only slightly slanted to give away that he was assessing me—whether to see if he could determine my character or my weaknesses, I wasn't sure. I held my breath wondering what he thought of me. Then I fought to keep my face neutral when the stupidest thought I'd ever had raced through my mind faster than I could stop it.

Did I make his breath catch the way he'd made mine?

He held out his hand. "Wyatt Jones."

His voice was deep, and my stomach did a swirl as I placed my much more delicate hand in his large, callused one and shook it firmly. A zing of electricity went through me at the touch, but I tried to keep myself composed so he wouldn't pick up on the way his handsomeness affected me. I knew better than most that looks didn't determine if someone was good at heart. His eyes widened with what looked like appreciation as he gave my hand a quick squeeze like he was impressed I gave a firm handshake. If he thought I'd give a wimpy handshake just because I was a girl, he was sorely mistaken.

I was a businesswoman and I'd built an empire—even if most people downplayed my success by saying I just wrote clever songs and got on stage in glittery outfits. I knew the truth. I was a force to be reckoned with, and I'd learned long ago a firm, solid handshake could set the tone early on in a meeting. I was not a weak woman who was a pushover.

"Brynn Davis."

I pulled my hand back and didn't miss how he squeezed his hand once before relaxing it at his side and turning his attention to Stella who had started talking to him. I should've been paying attention, but all I could do was stare down at his hand and think about that moment in the Kiera Knightley version of *Pride and Prejudice* when Darcy helps her into the carriage and then walks away, seemingly composed until he flexes his hand.

I hadn't fully appreciated the hype around that moment, but I got it now. There was something that made your insides turn to mush when you watched a stoic man show even the slightest sign of weakness.

I swallowed hard and scanned over the definitely tailored suit up to dark eyes that carried a hint of amusement. My cheeks flushed at being caught checking him out, but I knew I was wearing enough makeup that he likely wouldn't be able to tell.

"Do you still have the letter?" he asked Stella.

"Yeah. We've kept all the physical items in the safe and printed screenshots of the text messages. The police said there wasn't much they could do but document everything. A lot of good that'll do us if he gets to her," she mumbled.

Stella was not a fan of how the police department had—or in this case, hadn't—handled the situation. Hence, why I shouldn't have been surprised that she'd gone straight to hiring a full-time bodyguard. I was even relieved she hadn't decided to go with the usual company we used because I was getting less and less pleased with their "protection" with each event they'd been hired to attend with me. I couldn't imagine feeling safe with them.

But of all the bodyguards in the world, did she have to hire the company with the sexiest bodyguard I'd ever seen? Surely there were men available who wouldn't eviscerate my panties with just one look.

Rule #4

DON'T LET ANYONE GET UNDER
YOUR SKIN

Brynn

There was something so attractive about this man's mouth. If only he wasn't being a domineering asshole.

For the last hour, all he'd talked about was what I couldn't do, where I couldn't go, and who I couldn't see unless he was with me.

Any attraction I'd felt had dried up, slowly but surely the longer he talked. I understood he was here for my protection, but for fuck's sake, couldn't he at the very least discuss it with me instead of laying down the law like I was some petulant teenager on house arrest? Yes, he was the expert, but it was *my* life.

"Could we add additional security personnel instead of cutting out the meet and greets? Those are important to my fans, and I don't want to disappoint them."

"I think they'll understand if you tell them it's a safety concern," he answered.

"You didn't answer my question." I held firm. Truth was, those meet and greets reminded me why I put myself out there the way I did. Meeting people who shared with me how my words had gotten them through a bad breakup, depression, or even saved their life was the only thing that made giving up my privacy worth it. They were the reason I kept recording music instead of hiding in a cabin in the mountains. I needed that reminder or else I was afraid the loneliness might eat me alive.

"You don't just do what you're told, do you?"

He wasn't going to like this, but it was better he learn early. "I'm not a puppet. I will work *with* you but I do not work for you. I would appreciate if we could discuss things instead of you just laying down the law. I understand and respect that this is your area of expertise, but at the end of the day it's my life and I've only got the one. I will not completely surrender my independence because of this psycho. Nor will I compromise what my fans have come to expect from me."

I wasn't going to needlessly sacrifice my safety. He probably thought I wasn't taking this seriously, but I was. There were just some things I couldn't give up if I wanted to keep my sanity intact throughout all this.

"We can hire additional security personnel and limit the number of the people in the room with me," I stated, making clear this was my decision to make.

Stella piped up. "Oh, we could even pitch it as an exclusive one-on-one instead of the usual groups. Each person can be vetted prior to entering the room."

My heart lifted with hope and I glanced back at Wyatt. His prominent brows were furrowed, his dark gaze staring intently at my face. "This is really that important to you?"

"Her fans live for it," Stella said, likely thinking that would sell the idea.

But I heard him clearly. He'd picked up on what I

hadn't said—it wasn't just for the fans, but for me. If he was that observant, then he deserved honesty. "Yes, it's that important to me."

He scrutinized me, and despite always getting picked apart by the press, I'd never felt so exposed as I did sitting across from Wyatt.

He dropped his gaze to the tablet he'd brought with him. "Fine. I'll add additional security, background checks for all VIP guests, and screenings prior to entry with you."

Stella stood up. "I'll go call the tour manager and explain the changes." She left the room, leaving Wyatt and me alone together for the first time since I'd met him.

Silence weighed down the air.

"Thank you," I said quietly, my gaze intent on his rugged face.

And just like that, the initial attraction was back. Maybe he wasn't as domineering as I'd thought. He was precise in his work and intent on making sure all areas where my safety was concerned had no gaps. I couldn't really fault him for that. I appreciated how seriously he took his job. His focus and determination were a turn-on, even though I knew without fail a guy like Wyatt would never mix business with pleasure. Truthfully, neither would I. I'd never found a previous bodyguard, personal trainer, or any male I worked closely with as attractive as I kept finding Wyatt.

I was going to have fantasies about that sharp jaw and what it might feel like beneath my lips. Or how his callused hands would feel running over the silky softness of my skin.

And that was going to be a problem.

He set down the tablet and then his brown eyes stared intently into my own. "Your safety is the most important thing here. We'll try the meet and greets, but if at any point your safety is at risk, I'll shut them down."

"Understood. I appreciate your willingness to discuss it."

The corner of his mouth tilted up in a smile, and my heart stuttered in my chest. If I thought this man was handsome before, it was nothing compared to what he looked like with the faintest hint of a grin. "Believe it or not, you're not the most difficult client I've ever worked with. What you're asking for is fair and you were right. I should've opened it up as a discussion instead of—how did you put it?—laying down the law."

A smile split my face. "I appreciate that. I hope you'll come to realize I'm not a diva."

Damn it, he was even man enough to admit when he was wrong. His attractiveness just skyrocketed.

His subtle grin faded as a seriousness washed over his handsome face. "I already know you're not."

For some reason, his comment hit me harder than it should've, and the smile I wore slipped off my face. My throat got tight as my nose tingled with the potential of tears. It had been a long time since I'd felt seen for who I really was instead of just the pop star persona that was pushed in the press constantly. It had also been a long time since a man looked at me like a person instead of with dollar signs in his eyes.

This time the silence that passed between us wasn't heavy like it had been before. It was electric, causing my skin to tingle and my stomach to tighten with all the things I shouldn't want.

Like his lips on mine.

His hands on my body.

His gaze locked on my face, seeing into the depths of my soul while he thrust inside of me.

I broke our stare off first, afraid of what he might see in my gaze. He was too observant. It was already becoming painfully clear I couldn't hide in plain sight with Wyatt like I could with everyone else.

My biggest concern now was how long it would take for him to see through the composed and professional business-woman to the lonely and scared woman I hid underneath. I would rather he caught on to how attracted I was to him before he caught on to the truth of how close I was to breaking down.

Rule #5

DON'T GET DISTRACTED ON
THE JOB

Wyatt

My focus should've been on the crowd in the front row, the people mingling or running around backstage, or the ones who walked in or out of the hallway that led from backstage to the dressing rooms.

It *should've* been on those things.

Instead, I kept getting distracted.

Brynn was captivating.

Pop music had never been my thing—I preferred a mix of country or old-school Eminem and Linkin Park, depending on my mood—but I could hardly look away from the stage, from where she performed. Her voice was unlike anyone I'd ever heard—a little raspy, but strong and steady when she hit her high notes. She could also belt out some notes that left no doubts she was a powerhouse of a singer.

Knowing she wrote most of her own songs also had me distracted. I kept wondering who they were about. Was it the ex that was all over the media supposedly broken-hearted about their breakup? I hoped they weren't. He may be crying to the media, but Raf had already looked into him, and he was hooking up with several women on a pretty regular basis since the breakup. He only seemed sad when he knew the press was around. He wasn't worth her time or heartache.

So who was she writing about?

I shouldn't care, but it was becoming obvious I was doing a lot of things I shouldn't be doing.

She belted out the last note of her song, and then her light laugh rang around the huge space through her microphone. Her smile was the widest I'd ever seen it as she waved to the cheering crowd before pointing to her dancers as they took a bow. Then she gestured to her band, and finally up to where I knew the technicians were for the lighting. With one last wave at the crowd, she ran offstage and straight toward me.

Well, not toward *me*—I just happened to be standing where I knew she'd come because I'd seen her follow this same routine for all seven shows she'd performed so far. As her bodyguard, I probably should've told her that routines were dangerous for her safety, but I also liked knowing exactly where she'd be at the end of every show.

An assistant was already rushing forward to hand her a water bottle that she took with a smile and a "thank you" before chugging it down. My eyes narrowed on the way her throat moved as she swallowed before moving up the long column of her neck to her face where her eyes were closed. I could practically see her shedding the performer persona she wore every night when she was on stage.

I knew she'd open her eyes and snap it back into place for the after-show VIP meet and greet, but this single moment after every show felt like some secret shared between the two of us—even if she had no idea I paid such close attention to her ritual.

Except this time when she opened her eyes, they found mine immediately. Our gazes locked, and something heady and dangerous passed between us. The moment felt like it stretched on, but with a single blink, she broke the connection and turned toward the assistant who was already yammering on about who the VIPs were tonight. Brynn's expression was back to all business, and I forced my gaze away from her to once again scan the backstage area and assess her safety. Had I missed anything in those few seconds that it'd felt like she'd held me hostage with that green gaze of hers?

I moved with her as we made our way down the hallway to her dressing room where she'd freshen up before meeting the VIPs, who'd all passed thorough background checks. Anyone who hadn't been willing to go through the new vetting process had been removed from the list. I did a quick check of the room to make sure no one had gotten back here while we'd been up front, and then stepped outside so she could do whatever she needed to do.

When the assistant stepped out, I stopped her. "Has she eaten anything in front of you?"

The assistant—whose name was Amanda—blinked up at me with wide eyes. "Uh, I don't know. Was I supposed to have a snack ready? That wasn't on my list that Stella left for me."

I frowned. They all made sure she was hydrated, but this wasn't the first show where I'd noticed she wasn't getting offered any snacks or food which I'm sure she needed after that performance. "Put it on your list," I told her, handing her a five-dollar bill from my pocket. "High protein snacks in the future, but for tonight, go down to the vending machine that's by the restrooms and get her whatever's healthiest."

I'd noticed Brynn followed a relatively strict and healthy diet and didn't want to ruin that, but I was worried about her not having enough fuel to keep going at this pace.

Amanda nodded like a bobblehead and then ran off in the direction of the vending machines. Brynn opened the door to her dressing room shortly after and gave me a quick nod before we headed toward the room that had been set up for the meet and greet.

I saw the change in her body the second before we entered. With an inhale, she pasted on a smile that could've looked genuine to others, but I'd been around her enough to know it wasn't. She smiled just a little too wide when she was faking it. Not that she didn't enjoy these moments with her fans—because there were times when her shoulders relaxed and her smile met her eyes as they brightened at whatever a fan was telling her—but for the most part, it seemed to drain her more than it inspired her.

I wasn't sure anyone noticed except me. I'd started to wonder if Brynn even noticed.

After the fifth VIP guest was through, Amanda handed Brynn a granola bar. Brynn's shoulders fell and relief filled her features. "How'd you know? Is it that obvious I'm starving?" she asked with a little laugh.

Fuck.

"Oh, Wyatt said you hadn't eaten. I've made a note to have high protein snacks for all future shows like he told me. So sorry I didn't notice. This was the healthiest thing in the vending machine downstairs."

Brynn had stopped looking at her as soon as she'd said my name. I should've told Amanda not to say anything. Brynn's brows furrowed slightly, and her head tilted an inch to the side as she stared at me, an unspoken question passing from her to me that I refused to answer. I'd had years of practice keeping my face neutral, and I needed every single one of those years to keep it still in this moment.

I wasn't supposed to care about whether or not she ate. I was just supposed to care if someone attacked her.

"Thank you," she said, her gaze still locked on mine before she looked at Amanda who was already nodding and walking off so that Brynn could meet with the next VIP.

The rest of the night passed by uneventfully, everything happening just like it usually did.

Except for the fact that Brynn kept looking over at me, especially every time she took a bite of the granola bar.

My gaze snagged on her lips as I watched her take the last bite, and my heart started racing in a way it never had before when I looked up and realized I'd been caught.

Rule #6

NEVER LOOK AT SOCIAL MEDIA
WHEN YOU'RE DOWN

Brynn

Stella was talking to me about our flight plans for tomorrow, but for once, I didn't hear a word she said. I was lost in thoughts over a freaking granola bar.

I'd kept meaning to bring up snacks to Stella, but I always forgot by the time we got done with everything and I was too tired to care. It was one of those things that fell off the priority list, especially when everyone was so on edge because of my stalker. And no one had seemed to notice—mainly because I did everything in my power not to add to anyone's plate unless it was absolutely necessary.

But Wyatt had noticed.

A riot of butterflies took flight in my stomach, and I placed my hand over it, curious if I could feel it from the outside the way it seemed to be consuming my insides.

"Are you feeling okay?"

His deep voice washed over me and caused arousal to pool in my belly below where the butterflies fluttered.

"I'm fine," I said, turning back to glance at him.

His gaze was already locked on my face, and the concern that made his brown brows furrow had my heart joining the mix of havoc that he was wreaking on my body.

When was the last time someone had noticed the little things? When was the last time someone had wanted to take care of me who wasn't on my payroll?

Except Wyatt was on my payroll. So, was this just part of his job?

The fluttering stopped and was replaced with a sick feeling in my stomach.

Somehow the thought that he only cared because I paid him to made my heart hurt. Maybe it was because he was doing far more than my last bodyguard or maybe I was just going through a quarter-life crisis.

Whatever the reason, I needed to get my head back on straight. Of course it hadn't meant anything to him. He was just doing his job, and I needed to focus on doing mine.

As we approached the suite, he stepped forward and unlocked the door. I stood in the hallway while he did a sweep of both rooms and then gave me the nod that every-thing was clear. I turned to Stella and tried to ignore the twinge of guilt when I realized she was still talking to me and I hadn't caught a single word.

I placed a hand on her arm. "I'm so sorry, Stella. Can we go over this all in the morning? I'm wiped and not focusing very well."

Her eyes widened. "Oh gosh, of course. You get some sleep and we'll debrief in the morning and go over next week's agenda."

I gave her a wan smile. "Thanks."

"Night!" she said as she spun on her heel and headed to her own room.

I locked the door behind her and let the weight of the

day drag my shoulders down. Leaning my forehead on the closed door, I shut my eyes and took a breath to center myself.

A throat cleared behind me, and I silently cursed myself for not remembering that I wasn't actually alone on this tour.

I pushed my shoulders back and spun around, meeting Wyatt's dark gaze. "Anything else you need from me tonight?"

His eyes narrowed slightly, but otherwise his face didn't change. After a pause he said, "No."

I hated how my stomach swooped just from the way this man looked at me. Like he could see right through all the makeup and costumes and fake smiles to my very soul.

I broke our gaze, afraid if I stared any longer I'd see him decide that I was lacking and give me that cool, stoic demeanor he wore every day.

"Okay, then I'm going to bed."

I walked toward my room, which happened to be next to his, but I knew he wouldn't go to sleep until I'd fallen asleep, just like he had every night before on this tour.

"Good night, Brynn." His deep voice washed over me, and my steps faltered for a second before I caught myself and made the slight misstep look purposeful.

"Good night," I said, not daring to look back.

I shut the door behind me and went through my usual nighttime routine on autopilot. I shouldn't want him to care more than his job required. He may be insanely attractive, competent, and considerate of others, but he was my body-guard. He was off-limits and my life was already under scru-tiny. The last thing I needed was a rumor going around about us.

I got into bed, but no matter what position I got into, I

couldn't get comfortable enough to fall asleep. My mind was buzzing and my body felt almost restless. It wasn't unusual to be buzzing from endorphins and adrenaline after a show, but usually the ritual of my nighttime routine managed to calm me enough that I could sleep. I rolled over to the nightstand and grabbed my cell phone to pull up a meditation app.

Except my gaze caught on my social media app and I clicked on it instead. I knew it was a mistake almost instantly. There was a reason I'd hired a social media manager whose sole responsibility was running all my accounts. I rarely checked any of them myself unless I was doing a live or something. It seemed my social media manager had been earning her pay. I figured the vitriol from my ex's growing fan base was going to be bad, but I had no idea it was *this* bad. My posts were filled with nasty comments about my body—although they couldn't seem to decide whether I was a "fat bitch" or a "skinny whore."

My gaze caught on the most recent comment on my latest post.

You deserve to be alone. No one will ever luv you cuz ur a stuck-up b!tch who thinks she's better than everyone.

I dropped the phone on my stomach and stared at the white ceiling of my hotel room as my heart ached in my chest, not because the comment was mean—I was used to that—but because she'd voiced my own fears. I was worried the price of my fame was that I'd never find someone who loved me for me.

My whole body felt heavy. So heavy I wondered if it was possible for the weight of everyone's expectations and thoughts about me to weigh so much that I would fall through the bed, the hotel, and deep into the earth.

If I said that out loud, the media would have a field day calling me dramatic. Everything I did, every thought I had, every single second of my life was picked apart with a microscope. It's like they forgot there was an actual person underneath the fancy clothes and makeup.

I had a heart. I had feelings. But if I pointed that out, then I was the villain looking for attention. It was a lose-lose situation.

Which only made this insane crush I'd developed on my bodyguard even more of an impossibility. Not because of what they'd say about me—because it was already clear I couldn't do anything right as far as the media was concerned—but because they'd tear Wyatt down, and he didn't deserve that. He didn't deserve to live under a microscope and have all his past actions called into question.

I plugged my phone back in and set it back on the nightstand, then rolled over and pulled the sheets over my head. I could hide under here even if only temporarily. Under the covers in the dark, I could let myself feel the warmth I'd felt when I thought Wyatt cared...just because. I could pretend even though it was stupid to feed the fantasy about him when it could never go anywhere.

It was the memory of Wyatt's dark eyes and brows furrowed in concern that finally pulled me into a deep sleep.

Rule #7

CLOSE THE DOOR WHEN YOU WANT PRIVACY

Brynn

One Week Later

My skin hummed with the leftover adrenaline after an incredible show. It was always this way after I performed, like my skin was covered in buzzing bees without the threat of stinging. Just that intense rumbling hum. Tonight's show had been even more of a high than the past handful because the audience was feeling every song in a way that raised the energy in the venue.

I knew just based on how I was practically vibrating that my usual nighttime routine wouldn't be enough. I'd told myself I wouldn't fantasize about Wyatt anymore, but my guard was down and I couldn't stop thinking about what he'd look like completely naked. Between my legs. On top of me. Any position would suffice.

God, I bet this man was totally the kind of guy who would give a woman multiple orgasms.

While I personally had never experienced multiples

with a partner, there was something about Wyatt Jones that told me he'd deliver in spades. Maybe it was the confident way he carried himself, the slight swagger in his walk, even when his face was serious and he was all business.

What would it take to make him crack the tough façade?

We walked silently down the hall to my suite, the sound of our shoes brushing against the carpet and the ding of an elevator the only noises around. It was the first time we weren't surrounded by my entourage. Usually, I'd have Stella and her assistant with me. Sometimes it would be members of my band if we needed to fix things before the next show, or my tour manager, or any number of my staff. But tonight it was just Wyatt and me. For some reason, that made my heart giddy like I was being walked home by a date.

How ridiculous was that?

He had a room in my suite because it was part of Carmichael Security's procedures that he be close to me at all times, but he was always awake when I went to bed and dressed and ready by the time I woke up, so I wasn't sure if he even used the room. Stella hadn't been feeling well, so I'd made her go lie down, and everything had gone so smoothly tonight that most of my backup dancers and band were out partying. Wyatt hadn't felt confident about security while barhopping, and I hadn't fought him—or explained that I was never invited to those things anyway—since a night soaking in a bubble bath sounded infinitely better than going out.

We reached my suite, and he stopped right by the side of my door, allowing me to brush my keycard against the lock. It clicked and I pushed it open and stepped inside, pausing right past the threshold like he'd trained me to do—whether I opened the door or he did, I always had to wait at the entryway so he could do his thing. He was right behind me and did a sweep of the suite before he came back into the living room and gave me a nod.

"I need to step out to make a call, so I'll be right outside the suite if you need me."

"Okay," I said, feeling suddenly shy which, again, was ridiculous. I'd run circles around men in my industry and was a powerhouse. I hadn't felt shy around a guy since I was fourteen.

I needed to do something about these feelings that had me behaving completely out of character. Without another word to Wyatt, I went to my room and straight through to the attached bathroom. I started the water, then poured in my favorite hibiscus bubble bath I'd gotten on a trip to Hawaii once and had fallen instantly in love with. While the tub filled with hot, bubbly water, I stripped out of my clothes and then padded out to my suitcase to grab my favorite travel-sized bullet vibrator that thankfully was waterproof.

If I couldn't get multiple orgasms from my hunk of a bodyguard, then I needed to give them to myself so I'd stop losing my head around him and could focus on business. Plus, I'd learned my orgasms could be even more intense when I was running on post-show adrenaline.

The water was borderline too hot, but I slowly submerged my body anyway. The burn of the heated water made my muscles tighten before releasing their tension. Sagging against the rounded back of the oversized tub, I took my first relaxed breath all day. Maybe longer. My body became a limp noodle as the warmth seeped into my bones, and the water level rose until the bubbles covered my full breasts. I turned off the water by pushing the handle up with my toes. I was too relaxed to lean forward and use my hands.

But not too relaxed to forget the plans I had or ignore the way all my adrenaline was moving to that pleasure spot between my legs as my anticipation grew. I turned the vibe on with one hand and ran it slowly—seductively—around one breast, then the other. My nipples beaded painfully tight when I brushed the lowest vibration over them and imagined it was Wyatt's lips brushing over them. My clit pulsed with need between my legs, and a sense of urgency made my heart beat faster. I wasn't sure how much time I'd have before Wyatt returned. Moving the vibe down my stomach and across the trimmed strip of hair there, I finally reached my clit. My back arched slightly as I sucked in a sharp breath, the feeling gentle, but still intense after going so long without an orgasm. I hadn't had sex in months, and I hadn't self-pleasured myself in weeks because of everything we'd been dealing with between the stalker and my tour.

I needed this. I needed the kind of release I could only get with a good orgasm.

With one press on the side button, I increased the intensity and tossed back my head as pleasure coiled tight in my stomach.

"Oh God," I moaned, closing my eyes and pulling up the fantasy that had played on repeat in my dreams every night for the past week.

Wyatt kissed down my neck, murmuring against my skin. "Fuck, you're incredible. You're going to be a good girl and take my big, thick cock, aren't you?"

"Yes," I whimpered.

"It's going to be a tight fit, but I know you can do it."

"Mmm," I moaned.

His fingers moved down to rub small, gentle circles over my throbbing clit. "So wet for me."

"All for you."

"Mm, you have no idea what that does to me, to know you get this wet for me. I can't wait to taste this sweet pussy. It's my pussy now, isn't it?"

"Yesss," I stuttered as he replaced his finger with his mouth, sucking on my clit until stars burst across my vision.

"Wyatt," I moaned louder than I meant to as my back arched off the white porcelain of the tub and my orgasm crashed over me. It was fitting that I came so quickly, since even my dreams hadn't gotten me to feel his cock.

The aftershocks pulsed through me, each one making my breath ragged until I finally found the strength to turn off the vibe and drop it over the side of the tub onto the small, plush towel I'd put down.

Then a groan came from my bedroom and I sat up, staring through the bathroom door I'd left open to where Wyatt stood in the doorway of my bedroom—a door I had definitely forgotten to close.

Oh shit.

Wyatt and I stared at each other, the tension arcing across the room so thick, you could cut through it with a knife. My heart jackhammered in my chest. No, no, no. He was never supposed to see me. The layout of that room had the door only a handful of feet from a direct view into the bathroom. He could see everything above the surface of the water—thank God for thick bubbles blocking the rest of his view. But there was no way he'd missed me dropping my vibrator onto the towel. I held my breath, staring at him and waiting for him to say something. Anything.

His eyes narrowed and without a word, he spun around,

slamming the door closed behind him. I stared where he'd just been as the water cooled around me, but my cheeks were hot enough to keep me warm as mortification washed over me like a tidal wave.

What the fuck just happened?

Rule #8

DON'T COME THINKING ABOUT
YOUR CLIENT

Wyatt

This woman was going to be the death of me.

I did a quick check of the doors to make sure they were locked—both the main entry and the balcony door—because I was first and foremost a professional.

But I couldn't ignore my body for long, and the second I made sure things were clear, I went straight to my room. I didn't have a lot of time for this, but I needed to take care of the situation below my belt if I was going to be able to face Brynn with the same impassivity I'd had since I started working for her. A cold shower would've been the smarter move, but I'd already tried that several times over the last few weeks and knew it wouldn't do a damn thing to sate the burning hunger she'd unleashed in me since the first moment we met.

Her beauty was seductive, but it was working with her —watching how her mind worked, seeing the ways she always cheered on those around her and gave them credit, the way she interacted with her fans, all of it—that turned me on more than anything else. She was also incredibly smart, something I'd noticed she downplayed more often than not.

Undoing my belt buckle and shoving my shirt up my chest, I quickly took myself in hand, tugging up as I tipped my head back against the door and closed my eyes. Instantly, the image of Brynn with her head tilted back and her beaded nipples tipped up out of the bubbly water popped in my head. Her panting breaths, the not-so-subtle movement of her arm as her hand did something I couldn't see beneath the bubbles, the way her shoulders rolled back, lifting her chest farther out of the water as she cried out *my name*.

A low grunt escaped as I came too fast to the memory of her sweet voice saying my name in the throes of her orgasm. I slowed my motion as I let the pleasure linger, until a shiver zipped down my spine. It had been a few months since I'd last had sex, but fuck, that was embarrassingly fast. So fast, I was almost disappointed I didn't have a good excuse to keep picturing the subtle details I'd cataloged as I'd watched Brynn. I'd stood in that doorway far too long—even after it became clear what she was doing. Staring down, I huffed out a breath at the mess covering my stomach, glad I'd had the wherewithal to pull my shirt up. If I changed clothes, that would be too obvious, and when I walked out of this room, I had to pretend I hadn't watched Brynn bring herself to orgasm thinking about me.

I had to pretend she didn't affect me at all, which couldn't be further from the truth. No woman—especially not a client—had ever brought up such an insane mix of emotions in me.

I'd always prided myself on my professionalism. It wasn't like Brynn was the first beautiful celebrity I'd protected—not even close—but she was the first one I'd ever fantasized about. She was the first one I'd ever cared about more than I should, more than was strictly professional—like whether or not she ate or got enough sleep to go at the pace she did every day. It was unsettling to be thrown off-kilter by not only a client but a woman who was also a good thirteen years younger than I was.

I'd teased my brother, Travis, relentlessly when he started dating his daughter's best friend who was twenty years younger than he was, and I could already imagine the ways he'd tease me back if he found out the predicament I'd landed in.

Reaching over to the box of tissues on the dresser, I grabbed several and cleaned myself up before I pulled my shirt back down and finished putting myself back to rights. I faced the door and squared my shoulders, ready to field a bunch of questions from Brynn, or at the very least her profusely apologizing for getting caught.

She was beautiful, but she wasn't the type to throw herself at her bodyguard. I'd known plenty of those in my time in this profession. Brynn impressed the hell out of me, and maybe that was why my body responded to her in a way it never had to a client. She hadn't been afraid to speak up in our initial meeting, and not in a way that was bossy or bitchy. It was professional, while also making it clear she wouldn't just sit back and take being told what to do.

I shook my head and braced for the conversation I knew was coming. But when I opened the door, all was silent. Her bedroom door was still closed from when I'd shut it behind me, and no light came from beneath the door. I walked over to her door and knocked to make sure she hadn't left the suite. I didn't think so because she took her safety seriously and knew not to leave without me, but I needed to be sure.

"Yeah?" Her soft, sweet voice came through without any of the hesitation I would've expected after what had happened not even ten minutes ago.

"Just wanted to make sure you were in there," I called through the door.

"Yep. I'm going to sleep. Bright and early day tomorrow."

I frowned at the door. I mean, she *did* have an early day, but was she really going to pretend I hadn't seen her?

Maybe I should go with it and follow her lead. I could pretend as well as anyone. With one last glance at her door, I made my way back to my room. I wasn't a heavy sleeper, but I still slept with the door open to make sure I could hear if anything was amiss.

But as it turned out, I didn't need the door open because I barely slept a wink, my mind swirling with different variations of what had happened, only with a different ending—one where she came on my cock instead of on her hand and I came inside her instead of on my stomach.

***

I was already dressed and sitting at the table in the dining room of the suite with coffee and trays of breakfast food laid out when Brynn walked out wearing what looked like men's boxers and an oversized Paramore T-shirt. Her reddish brown hair cascaded down her back in that messy bedhead way that somehow on her still looked sexy.

At that particular thought, I glanced down at the newspaper in front of me, keeping my body still, so she wouldn't look over here and catch a glimpse of the bulge in my jeans. I was used to wearing suits on the job—something Raf had always stipulated. But Brynn had made it clear she wanted me to dress casual, and after discussing it with Raf, we agreed that in this case the client would get what they wanted.

She covered her mouth as she yawned and then mumbled, "Morning."

"Good morning."

She grabbed a croissant and tore off a chunk before shoving it into her mouth. I'd expected her to sleep in silk negligees and only eat fruit for breakfast, but had been pleasantly surprised when I found out she was a sucker for carbs in the morning. She set the croissant on her plate and reached for a waffle.

"Want some coffee?" I asked.

My chest tightened when she gave me a soft grateful smile. "That would be great. Thanks."

I poured her a cup, passing her the cream and sugar and wondering when this woman would prove that she was like all the other celebrities I'd protected—not that they were all superficial, shallow socialites, but most were.

She took a sip of her coffee after she'd doctored it with plenty of sugar and a splash of cream, and I watched with fascination as she closed her eyes, hummed low in her throat, and sagged back in her chair. "God, that's good."

I imagined her saying that about something else entirely and then immediately forced myself to look back at the newspaper.

"Should we go over the agenda for today?" she asked.

Clearly she wasn't going to bring up what happened last night, and while it was tempting to follow her lead, I also needed to clear the air so we could maintain professionalism. "Actually, I wanted to talk about last night."

Her cheeks flushed pink, but she maintained eye contact, and my respect for her grew.

"I'm sorry for not closing the door," she said.

I heard what she didn't say. She wasn't sorry for masturbating. She wasn't sorry for coming with my name on her lush, pink lips. She didn't say it like a come-on, but it affected me like one.

I kept my expression neutral even as my pants grew uncomfortably tight.

"I wanted to make it clear that I am here for your protection, but that's all." This wasn't the first time I'd had to tell a female client I wouldn't cross the professional boundaries in place. My brother and I had been getting in trouble with girls our whole lives. Everyone had told us we were too good-looking for our own good.

But I would never cross that line at work. I'd never risk losing my place with Raf's company. He'd given me purpose after I'd left the military, and I respected him and the business he'd built way too much to break his rules.

No client was worth that risk. Not even one as beautiful and unique as Brynn.

"I understand," she replied. "And I respect your role as my bodyguard. I'm sorry if I made you uncomfortable." Remorse coated her words and filled her eyes.

But again, I caught what she *didn't* apologize for.

Clearing my throat, I nodded once, and then went over the security plans for today. I'd made myself clear, and she seemed to respect that, even if it was clear she wasn't sorry for her actions.

I was confident this wouldn't be an issue in the future.

Rule #9

DON'T WASTE TIME ON UNREQUITED CRUSHES

Brynn

Three Weeks Later

I waved one last time to my fans as I rushed off the stage, followed by my dancers. They went left backstage, and I went right where Wyatt stood sentry as he did during every show. My core clenched as my gaze dropped down his tall, fit body. This man had looked fine as hell in a suit, but the blue button-down and khakis he was wearing tonight were doing something dangerous to me. Every night after a show, this man tempted me like no one else ever had.

He'd laid down the law three weeks ago, and I had every intention of respecting the boundaries he put in place. But you know what they say about the road to hell... I was pretty sure I was on my way there if the dirty images my mind was creating were any indication. I hadn't apologized for masturbating to the image of him, but I was sorry he caught me. Okay, maybe not one hundred percent sorry since the thought of him watching me had now played on an endless loop in my head whenever I was lying in bed waiting for sleep to pull me under.

I'd never masturbated in front of someone else before, and even though it hadn't been intentional, there was something invigorating about knowing his eyes were on me while I made myself come. And now I couldn't stop thinking about doing it again while he watched. There was something about the ultimate trust you had to give that person to not sit there and laugh at you or judge you, but to just watch you enjoying yourself. I couldn't think of a single partner from my past I would've wanted to watch me, but the thought of Wyatt watching me again never failed to make me wet.

Wyatt handed me a towel which I used to wipe off the excess sweat on my forehead from my performance. He'd caught on quickly that I always headed straight to the table backstage to grab one and wipe off. I don't know if he started holding it out to me to save us time or what, but I appreciated it more than he knew.

"Thanks," I said, glad I had my performance as an excuse for the heat in my cheeks, so only I knew it was really from the way this man affected me.

He gave me a silent nod and then his gaze was scanning the area around us. Wyatt was always observing our surroundings. I was sure he never missed a thing, except maybe my growing—and completely unrequited—crush on him.

I dabbed at my neck with the towel and took advantage of his focus being on the things going on around us. My gaze traced the sharp edge of his jaw, memorized how his dark eyebrows arched as his brown eyes narrowed on something to our left. His mouth was set in a line, and occasionally there was a slight tic in his jaw when he was especially focused. The only real indication of his age was the fine lines around his eyes. There were no signs of gray in his hair although I had no doubt this man would be an exceptionally sexy silver fox when the day came.

But as much as his face always mesmerized me, it was his hands that captivated and enticed me even more. He had thick veins along the backs of his hands, and his palms and fingers were callused. He was a man who had used his hands a lot, and I often wondered what he did in his spare time. Were the rough calluses from building something? Or from a career before he became a bodyguard?

I knew he was ex-special forces, but wasn't privy to the details of his time in the military. I had so many questions, and I couldn't ask a single one because it would cross a line that he had clearly drawn in the sand, as he should have.

He worked for me.

I needed to remember that he was a professional doing his job. The reminder finally sobered me up. I hated when people objectified me and yet here I was doing the exact same thing to him. I needed to get a hold of myself and treat him like I would any other employee that worked for me.

Thankfully, my backstage assistant chose that moment to come rushing over with a small bowl of almonds and a stick of string cheese. Every night since the night Wyatt had first asked her to get me a snack, she'd had something at the ready that my nutritionist would wholeheartedly approve of. She passed me the bowl and gestured for me to hand her my towel. I gave her a nod of thanks and then turned back to Wyatt.

"You ready?" he asked me, doing one last sweep before looking down at me.

I was not going to admire how tall he was.

I wasn't.

"Yeah, let's go," I said and then popped an almond in my mouth so I wouldn't say anything else.

We started walking toward the dressing room so I could change.

"Are you going out with the dancers?"

I paused, my steps stuttering slightly, but Wyatt—observant as always—caught it. Knowing he was watching my facial expression and could read me better than anyone else in my circle, I did my best to keep my face neutral. "The boss doesn't get invited to those things."

He frowned. "The barhopping a few weeks ago...?"

I shrugged. "I wasn't invited. You assumed, and I let you think what you wanted since you said no to it anyway."

He faced forward, but I caught his eyebrows slanted over his eyes in a stern frown like he was reorganizing information in his head. It was strangely endearing watching this man classify new facts in his brain. I could practically see the wheels turning.

I expected him to remain silent, but he surprised me. "You never go out much."

"No, I suppose I don't. Is that different from your other clients?"

"I'm not allowed to talk about other clients."

My heart sank a little at that. For a minute it had felt like we were bonding, and as much as I was trying to remind myself not to find him attractive, I couldn't deny it would be nice to feel like we were friends.

"But yes," he said, his voice lower as we reached my dressing room. I spun around to face him as I pushed the door open with one hand, my snack still held in the other. His brown gaze drilled into mine. "You're definitely different than I expected."

My heart caught in my throat. "A good different, I hope."

He didn't say anything, his gaze locked on mine for a second too long, and then he gave one nod and broke our stare. "I'll be out here when you're ready."

I swallowed thickly. "I'll be just a few minutes."

True to my word, I was changed and ready to head back to the hotel within five minutes. He gestured for me to walk and we fell in step together. The extra security at the venue pushed open the back door to where my car waited. Cameras flashed and I smiled and waved, prepared for this since they were always waiting after every show.

Even ten years into my career, it was still overwhelming to see all the flashing lights and hear the cacophony of voices screaming demands for my attention. Then there were all manner of things being shoved at me to sign.

I waved, but didn't stop. Wyatt's hand was braced at my back as he pushed his other hand out, using his body as a blockade around me.

A blur caught my attention a split second before a woman was moving forward and screaming at me. She moved to throw something at me at the same time that Wyatt hauled my body against his and spun us, protecting me with his body. The chaos lasted only seconds, security quickly catching the fan that rushed toward me, but as I glanced up into Wyatt's fierce and protective gaze, time felt like it stopped altogether.

We were chest to chest, my nipples pebbled hard and pressed so tightly to him, there was no way he could miss them. Something sticky dripped on my hand that was partially on his hip, and when I pulled it closer, my heart sunk at the sight of red.

"Oh my God. Wyatt, you're bleeding." There was no

way he could miss the panic in my voice as I frantically tried to spin him around to see where he was hurt. But there was no moving a man as big and sturdy as he was unless he wanted to be moved. Instead, he grabbed my hands and held them against his chest.

"Brynn, look at me."

I looked up into his calm eyes. "I'm not hurt." He looked down at my hands, assessing the liquid, and then back at me. "This looks like red paint. I promise I'm fine."

The combo of the adrenaline from the show, the scare of the attack, and the terror that he could've been hurt made tears burn in my eyes.

His jaw clenched and his hands tightened on mine as we heard the other members of the security team handle the threat.

I'd told myself this was only a crush, but as he held my gaze, I knew my feelings had already become so much more than that.

I knew without a doubt that there was no way I could ever look at Wyatt as just my bodyguard. It was too late. I already cared about him more than was professional, more than I cared about most people in my life.

It was stupid for a million reasons, and completely one-sided, but I couldn't ignore the way this man made me feel anymore.

I just wished I wasn't the only one falling.

Rule #10

DON'T GET JEALOUS OF YOUR COWORKER

Wyatt

My self-control was failing, and as I held her tight to my body, everything fading away around us as I drowned in her green eyes, I wondered if maybe it would be worth it.

Not once had I ever considered crossing that line, but in this moment I was so close to saying "fuck it" and leaning forward to kiss her.

The terror—for me—in her eyes when she thought I'd been hurt had nearly sunk me to my knees. The way she fussed over me before I stilled her hands. The way she looked at me now like she'd be devastated if anything happened to me.

Maybe I'd already crossed the line because even the way I held her against me wasn't remotely close to being considered professional.

Then a flash went off in my periphery and I remembered where we were. Who she was. Who *I* was to her. And my professionalism kicked into overdrive.

I moved with her in my arms the few feet to the SUV

and placed her inside before I closed her door. Before walking all the way around to the passenger side, I stopped at the back to take off my jacket that I'd worn to conceal my gun and toss it in the trunk space since it was covered in red paint.

The driver was another guy who worked for Raf, and he'd already been briefed with our itinerary, something I was grateful for as my mind reeled with how I'd just behaved. That split second could've been enough for someone to hurt her if the threat had been real. What the fuck was I doing?

Maybe I should request a transfer to a different job. Even as the thought entered my mind, I immediately dismissed it. There was no way I could sit back and let someone else guard her. I was too invested, which I realized was a big reason why I should absolutely tell Raf to replace me. But I wasn't going to.

Brynn was *mine* to protect.

I glanced back and our gazes caught for a second before she turned her head to look out the window, her reddish-brown hair pulled back into a high ponytail. Every time we passed a streetlight, it would illuminate the pensive look on her face as she stared absently out the window at the passing scenery.

Fuck, she was pretty. So pretty it almost hurt to look at her.

I faced forward, refusing to let my thoughts spiral more out of control. I was grateful we were in New York tonight because Raf had an extension team here, and there was a replacement for me waiting at the hotel. Raf had even offered me his extra condo to stay in tonight since he was still in LA. It was something I knew he wouldn't typically offer his employees, but I wasn't just his employee—I was his friend.

His friend who'd almost crossed a line there was no going back from.

I was looking forward to a full night off. Maybe it would help me get my head straight if I wasn't around Brynn and her sweet scent—or the memory of her little bullet vibrator between her legs and my name on her lips which had haunted me for the last several weeks.

I'd never struggled so hard to focus on the job.

We arrived at the hotel, and I opened Brynn's door like I always did. She slid across the backseat and stepped out, but her foot must've gotten caught on something because she started to tip forward as if she was going to fall, and I quickly placed my hand on her belly to catch her while my other hand came out to grab hers. She looked up at me, those big green eyes once again holding me captive in all the ways they shouldn't.

"Okay?" I choked out, trying to remember she was a job.

Just a fucking job.

She cleared her throat. "Yeah, sorry."

I nodded and stepped back, removing my palm from her belly, while keeping my other hand tight around hers to help her the rest of the way out. The skin of the hand that had landed on her stomach tingled as if the nerves had been affected by touching her.

Isn't that always how I felt even at the simplest touch with her? What was it about her that caused this reaction when I'd never experienced it before in my life—with a client or otherwise?

We were silent as we walked into the hotel and up to her room where we'd be meeting my replacement for the night. My gut tightened the closer we got to her room, the idea of someone else watching her making me uneasy. What if something happened to her? What if he couldn't protect her the way I could?

It was a stupid thought. I knew Raf only hired the best guys who were thoroughly vetted, but I couldn't stop the thought no matter how hard I tried. When I saw the guy who'd be covering for me, I let out a breath I hadn't known I'd been holding.

"Hey man, I thought you were in Europe," I said to another one of my old Navy Seal buddies Jamie, who'd also been recruited by Raf. I swore he was single-handedly trying to hire our entire unit.

Jamie reached his hand out to shake mine. "Nah, came back early so I could relieve you. Raf said you'd probably be picky about who was covering for you."

"Is that right?"

I hoped my tone didn't give away how accurate that was. Hadn't I just been thinking about all the ways my replacement would be inadequate?

Jamie's brow arched at Brynn as his typical enigmatic smile graced his face. "And you must be Brynn Davis. Pleasure to serve you." He reached out a hand to shake hers, and she took it as professionally as she'd taken mine when we first met.

So why did that make my stomach burn with acid? She was being professional. He was being professional. I was the one being an asshole by standing here silently fuming with jealousy instead of making introductions and making sure she was comfortable with him.

Pulling my head out of my ass, I said, "Brynn, this is Jamie Walsh. He and I have worked closely together for years. You're in good hands tonight."

"Jamie, it's great to meet you. Hopefully, this will be a very boring night for you. I plan to go inside, drink some water, and go to bed."

"No ragers tonight, huh?"

Her lips tilted up in a smile, but her eyes wore the exhaustion she usually had by the time we got back to our suite after a show. "Not tonight. Or most nights for that matter. I'm not really a rager kind of girl."

He nodded like he understood exactly what she meant and then stepped back to let her into the room. I stayed out in the hallway, expecting her to go inside and close the door, but instead she stopped right at the threshold. She glanced back, those green eyes of hers piercing my heart.

"Good night, Wyatt. See you tomorrow."

"Good night, Brynn."

The door shut behind her, and instead of seeing if Jamie had caught on to anything, I slapped him on the side of his arm and started walking back toward the elevators. "See you bright and early, Lucky Charms."

Jamie's boisterous laughter filled the hall and brought a smile to my face as I entered the elevator to head to Raf's condo for the night.

Rule #11

BIG BROTHERS ALWAYS GIVE THE
BEST ADVICE

Wyatt

A text pinged on my phone as soon as I walked into Raf's condo. I threw the keys on the marble island and dug through my pocket for my phone, expecting it to be from Jamie about Brynn, but instead it was from my brother.

TRAVIS

Hey, call me when you get a chance.

I hit his contact and then put the phone on speaker while I moved through the kitchen to see if Raf had any food stocked in this place. Knowing him, he would've had a service come in and provide all my favorites even though I was only here for one night. He was too rich for his own good—old family oil money or something. He'd been stingy on the details of where his wealth came from, but I knew he had enough that he never had to work a day in his life if he didn't want to.

"Hey, I didn't expect you to call so quickly," my brother's voice rang through the silence.

"Yeah, you caught me at a good time. I've got the rest of the night off."

"You at Raf's place?" My brother knew and loved Raf.

"Yeah."

"Is it as nice as his LA place?"

"Smaller, but yeah, it's pretty much exactly what you would expect Raf to own."

"How's the job going?"

He knew I couldn't give details, but he always asked anyway. And for once, I was grateful he was bringing it up first because I needed some perspective from someone who'd been in a similar situation as far as crushing on a woman completely off-limits. Grabbing a beer from the fridge, I popped off the top and then leaned against the counter.

"Well, it's gotten a little...complicated."

He hesitated. "Complicated how?"

"I'm attracted to her."

Figured there was no point hemming and hawing with the truth. My brother knew how seriously I took my job and that I'd never do anything to sacrifice my position, so he'd also know if I was saying this, it wasn't as simple as basic attraction. It was deeper.

It was a feeling that clawed at my insides the more time I spent around her and the more I tried to ignore it.

"Hold on a sec," he murmured through the phone before I could hear the sound of a door closing in the background. "Okay, I'm not sure I heard you right. Did you say you were attracted to her?"

"Yeah." It felt good to admit it. I'd barely been able to admit it to myself, but saying it out loud unleashed it some-how. It made my chest expand as if a weight had been removed. "Don't worry, I'm probably not going to do anything about it."

It was the "probably" that told me I likely wouldn't remain professional if I had to work with her too much longer. Any other woman and the answer would've been a clear "Don't worry, I *won't* do anything." But I could no longer guarantee restraint with Brynn.

Tonight it had been especially hard not to give her comfort the way I knew she craved. I'd heard the loneliness in her voice when she admitted the boss doesn't go out with the dancers. Pairing that with the knowledge that she'd spent every night of the tour either surrounded by people she paid or completely alone only reinforced that loneliness. And then holding her in my arms when that fan rushed her —it shouldn't have felt so good. She shouldn't have fit perfectly against me. Time shouldn't have felt like it slowed down when she was in my arms the way it had during those few seconds that felt like minutes.

I shouldn't hate that another man was protecting her right then when I had this insane feeling that I should be the only one guarding her.

"How did you know with Sadie?" I asked my clearly speechless brother. He was likely waiting for me to tell him I was just kidding.

Joke was on him this time.

"She's younger, isn't she?" He knew I wouldn't tell him who she was, not while she was my client.

I took a swig of my beer and then gripped the back of my neck. "She's thirteen years younger."

He chuckled. "After you gave me all that shit for Sadie, this feels a little like Karma."

"Yeah, I'm aware, but maybe you can tease me endlessly

about it later. I'm slipping here, Trav. I've never crossed that line."

"I know," he said, his tone more somber.

"But this woman, she's…fuck, she's nothing like I expected when I got the profile on her from Raf. I expected her to be stuck-up, full of herself, vapid, and shallow."

"But she's not?"

"Not even fucking close. She's smart, like crazy smart. She's built this huge business and she's incredible at what she does. She's always striving to be better and thinking about how she can best take care of her team. She's kind to people who can do nothing for her, and yet not soft or a pushover. She's impressive as hell."

"Okay, but what makes you think you might cross that line? It's one thing for you to be interested, but if she's as smart as you say, surely she's not looking to cross that line, or she might even have a partner already."

"She's single, completely single, and…" My brother and I didn't really go into details about our sex lives, especially now that he was married to Sadie, his daughter Jenna's best friend.

"And?" he prompted.

"And there was maybe a…" How the hell did I explain catching her fantasizing about me? "An incident."

"Incident? Wyatt, you're gonna need to give me more than that because my mind is going in a million directions at the moment."

I rubbed my eyes. "I caught her touching herself and she said my name."

There was a moment of silence and then, "Woah."

"Yeah."

"Okay, so not one-sided."

"Safe to say it's probably not, but I also think we both know we can't really cross that line."

"When should I start calling you Kevin Costner?"

I couldn't have rolled my eyes harder than I did then. "How long have you been holding on to that *Bodyguard* reference?"

"Pretty much since you started working for Raf. Actually, probably before you started working for him, but after he announced he was opening a security company for executive protection."

I remembered that barbecue at my brother's house when Raf told us his plans. Travis had asked him what exactly "executive protection" meant and Raf had said it was essentially bodyguards.

"Anyway...getting back to the problem. Got any brotherly advice for me?"

He chuckled, and it was clear he was back to finding this situation hilarious. "Wear a condom."

"Seriously?"

"Come on, Wyatt, I don't know what you expect me to say. You've never come to me with this kind of issue, so I assume that if you're asking for my advice it means you've already crossed the line in your mind."

"I haven't."

Had I?

I definitely had when I'd thought about her after I caught her masturbating. And that wasn't the last time I thought about her while I jacked off.

Fuck.

"I gotta go," I told him, needing to end this conversation and think long and hard about what I was really risking here.

I hung up and left my phone on the counter as I headed

into the bedroom. I was already too tempted to text Jamie and check in, so it was safer to have my phone a far distance from me.

The bedroom was as extravagant as the rest of the place. I'd never stayed in Raf's New York condo since I usually stayed on the West Coast, but I definitely understood the appeal and why he took so many trips here. If I thought the bedroom was nice, it was nothing compared to the bathroom.

After a long day, a shower to loosen up the tension in my muscles was a great idea. It was one of those fancy rain showers along with three different showerhead features if you didn't want to use the rain one. I turned it up as hot as my skin could tolerate and then stripped out of my clothes unceremoniously, dropping them in a heap on the floor before I stepped inside.

The second the hot water hit my body, my muscles relaxed. I let the warmth seep into my bones then rinsed my hair. As soon as I closed my eyes to avoid getting water in them, I saw Brynn. Those big green eyes, her brown hair that had naturally reddish streaks in it. Just the image of her in my mind was enough for my body to react. All the blood rushed south, and instead of feeling shame or guilt, I gave in.

I gripped my hard shaft, tugging a few times as I let my imagination go wild with images of Brynn—some from that night I caught her in the bath, some from her performances, and some that had never happened, but that I'd give my left nut to experience in real life.

My grip tightened as my strokes increased. I braced my other hand against the smooth black tile of the shower, and I imagined Brynn down on her knees.

Her plump pink lips wrapped around the thick head of

my cock. Her green eyes looked up at me, watching intently for further instruction.

"Suck it."

My head tipped back as she sucked hard, her tongue flicking lightly underneath and making pleasure tingle up my spine.

"Fuck, that's it. Just like that."

But Brynn was an overachiever and she wanted more. She gripped my thighs as she took more of me into her mouth until I hit the back of her throat. She swallowed, her throat tightening around the head of my dick.

"You're such a dirty girl, aren't you," I said, locking my gaze with hers and brushing her wet hair out of her face. "You've convinced everyone you're a good girl, but you love having me at the back of your throat, don't you? You like being on your knees while I fuck that dirty little mouth of yours, don't you?"

Her eyes watered as I pumped faster into her mouth and she hummed a confirmation. The vibration of her hum combined with her swallowing again was all it took.

I came with a deep groan against the tile wall. I dropped my forehead against the back of my hand still braced against the tile as I struggled to find the strength to remain standing.

If just the fantasy of this woman left me feeling this wrecked, how would I feel if I got to experience the real thing?

Rule #12

DON'T MAKE BIG DECISIONS WHEN YOU'RE EMOTIONALLY INVESTED

Wyatt

Nothing should've surprised me anymore, but when Grant Davis—the same Grant Davis who worked with my sister-in-law, Sadie—answered Brynn's hotel room door instead of Jamie, I could safely say I was surprised.

"Grant?"

He smiled wider. "Hey Wyatt. Come on in," he said as he stepped back.

I spoke as I looked for Jamie, who should've been the only one to answer the door. "What are you doing here?"

"I'm in town for an architecture conference and wanted to see my baby sister."

I stopped in my tracks and spun to face him. I knew Brynn had an older brother, but somehow it hadn't clicked that her brother was a man I already knew fairly well from times Sadie had invited him to barbecues at their house.

He looked nothing like Brynn. Where she had green eyes and reddish-brown hair, he had sky-blue eyes and pitch-black hair. Maybe that was why I never put two and two together.

And then everything clicked. "You knew about Carmichael Security from Connor."

Connor was Grant's best friend and another bodyguard for Carmichael Security. He was also married to my niece, Jenna. Grant nodded. "Yeah, when Brynn told me about the stalker, I immediately recommended to Stella that she reach out to Carmichael for protection. I would've insisted Connor guard her, but I know there's no way he'd take a job that would have him all over the world for the next several months with Jenna due in just a few weeks."

He stepped closer and lowered his voice. "I'm glad it's you, though. I know Raf only hires the best, but it eases some of my worries knowing you personally, and knowing you take your job seriously and won't let this psycho get to her."

Years of training were the only reason my face remained neutral when instead I wanted to wince. If he only knew the thoughts I'd had about his sister last night—and most nights over the last several weeks—he'd be punching me in the face instead of looking at me with gratitude. They had been anything but professional.

But I was saved from having to respond by Jamie coming out of a side room with a very distraught looking hotel manager. Brynn came out behind them, fresh-faced and looking infinitely more beautiful without all the makeup on that she wore for her shows. But then my gaze caught on the way she worried her lip between her teeth and the faintest hint of blue under her eyes as if she hadn't gotten enough sleep.

"What's going on?" I asked.

Jamie answered, holding out a folded piece of paper.

"Grant arrived at the same time as the room service breakfast order, with a note attached that Grant thought was from the hotel."

Grant's smile dropped as his gaze darted between Jamie, Brynn, and the hotel manager. "It wasn't someone from the hotel?"

Jamie never looked away from my face, even as he answered Grant. "'Fraid not."

That was all the prompting I needed to unfold the thick paper, not quite card stock, but not standard printer paper either. My heart stopped as my brain processed the typed words on the page.

Careful what you ingest. I've heard croissants could give you a heart attack. Enjoy your meal.

Bile rose in my throat, and the usual calm, collected demeanor I typically embodied was nowhere to be found. "Did you pull cameras on the kitchen? Who had access to her order?"

Jamie stepped forward, lowering his voice to keep it between us. "This isn't my first rodeo, Cap," he said, using my old Seal nickname—a shortened version of Captain America. Then louder for the others, "The hotel manager has already given us full access to the cameras. There are no signs of anyone besides hotel staff. We called down and ordered the usual breakfast spread. The kitchen has the ticket for that order, but then all that was delivered was a tray of croissants and this note. I'm planning to go downstairs and talk to the staff right now with the hotel manager. I've already bagged the croissants and we'll get them tested for poison."

"This guy knows where she is. How is that possible? No

one else on her team is staying at this hotel. She's using a new fake name, and the only people who were supposed to know she was here at all are in this room."

Jamie's eyes narrowed. "I understand the severity of the situation. I have the same questions you do, but barking at me won't get you answers any faster."

Had I been "barking" at him, as he so eloquently put it? Maybe. But she was supposed to be safe here. It was the only reason I'd taken the night off to get a full night's sleep.

Then I finally looked at Brynn. She had her arms crossed as she stared out vacantly at the city. The sun was still rising, and it bathed the skyscrapers with a pink and orange glow. New York City didn't seem quite as chaotic as it normally did. No, instead all the chaos was in this room. And instead of adding to it, instead of freaking out like other celebrities I'd worked with, she was calm, still, frozen.

When was I going to finally stop comparing her to other celebrities? She wasn't like them. She wasn't like anyone. She was just her. Beautiful, brilliant, brave.

This guy had been slowly escalating for months, and in just the six weeks I'd been working with her, I'd not heard her complain once. All she'd done was make sure none of the added security ruined the experience for her fans.

Everyone was worried about Brynn Davis, the pop star —including Brynn herself—but were any of them worried about *Brynn*? Had any of them thought about how this was affecting her as a person? Even in just the time I'd been working with her, I'd noticed how she'd closed in on herself. She needed a break from the madness that had become her life—and not just the stalker, but the media blitzes, the concerts night after night.

She deserved a chance to breathe away from the chaos.

"After tonight's show, there's a two-week break. We

were planning to go back to LA, but if her stalker can find her here, then her house isn't safe," I said aloud, my gaze still trapped on Brynn. She finally looked away from the window and at me. Her eyes were pinched with fear, longing, loneliness, and something deeper—something I couldn't name and I wasn't entirely certain she could either.

"Agreed," Jamie said with a nod. "We'll need to find a safe house for her. I can call Raf to see if he's got something."

A thought was already brewing in my mind. One of our old Seal buddies had made a ton of money on the stock market and bought a house on Lake Tahoe. He was always telling us we could borrow it anytime we wanted.

I knew for a fact he'd used Raf for the added security, which meant it would be safe for her.

"I've got a place. I just need to clear it with Raf."

Rule #13

DON'T MAKE ASSUMPTIONS

Brynn

The cabin Wyatt took us to was right on Lake Tahoe, and even though it was a relatively small A-frame, it was clearly remodeled with modern amenities and high-tech security. There was an outdoor sauna and hot tub set off to the right, and the entire front of the cabin was a wall of windows that had the same mirrored protective film on the outside that I had on the windows in my house so no one could see inside, but without obstructing the views.

We walked inside and Wyatt dropped our bags next to the door and propped his large hands on his trim hips. He looked around the space with such focus it was as if he was cataloging every inch. A smile tugged at the corner of my lips as I followed his lead.

The wall of windows directly in front of us faced out to the pristine blue lake. It was so breathtaking, I almost didn't want to tear my gaze away, but the rest of the cabin called to my curiosity. To the right of the windows was a short book-shelf, probably because of the steep tilt of the roof since I doubted much else would fit there. Centered on the right wall was a stone fireplace with a stack of wood already waiting for us. I couldn't remember the last time I saw a fireplace that took wood and wasn't turned on with the push of a button. There were stairs to the right of the fireplace that went up to a loft room. Even from down here, I could tell there was only one bed. Unless there was an extension somewhere, it looked like the sleeping situation would be interesting. Beneath the loft was the kitchen, and tucked to the side was the bathroom. A plush, expensive-looking brown couch sat along the wall opposite the fireplace. It looked like the perfect place to curl up with a book and read or stare out at the lake.

Wyatt hummed low in his throat, a frown on his handsome face. He bent down to pick up my bags and proceeded to walk up the stairs to the loft. "You can have the bed. I'll sleep on the couch," he called down, although in the small space, he probably could've whispered and I would've heard him clearly.

It was becoming clear that there would be very little privacy between us for as long as we were here. I wondered how long it would take before my resolve to remain professional with Wyatt flew right out the window. I'd seen the way he looked at me when he'd held me against his body after that fan rushed me, and it wasn't the way any other bodyguard had.

It was full of hunger and desire, but not with the added gleam of wondering what I could do for him like men I'd dated in the past. The reason it had been easy to be single for so long was because most men from my previous relationship had used me as a stepping stone for their own fame or careers.

But not Wyatt.

I suspected he was fighting the same intense pull I was. Now we would be trapped in this small cabin in the woods for the next two weeks, and I wasn't sure I could ignore my attraction to him for that long.

He came back down the stairs and looked around again, like he was at a loss for what to do now.

His dark brown eyes landed on me, and I realized it was the first time he'd looked me in the eye since we got here. "Are you hungry?"

For you? Yes.

"Not really." I hadn't had much of an appetite since New York, something he'd noticed because he was constantly asking me if I was hungry or putting snacks—my favorites, even though I'd never told him what my favorites were—in front of me.

"Are you sure? I had the fridge and cabinets stocked before we got here."

"I'm sure. Thank you though."

I paused. Was this the first time I'd thanked him?

"I'll grab us waters at least," he said, heading to the kitchen.

I stepped forward and grabbed his arm, stopping him in his tracks. "Thank you, Wyatt. For all you've done over the last several weeks. I haven't said it enough, but I appreciate it. I appreciate *you*." My voice had gotten lower by the time I finished talking, and I was sure he could see my heart in my eyes the way I was looking at him.

"Of course. It's my job," he said, his voice lower than normal, but his words were enough of a jolt that I instantly dropped my hand and nodded like he hadn't just hurt my feelings.

It was the reminder I needed. It was the reminder he shouldn't have had to give in the first place. Again.

This was just a job to him. *I* was just a job.

Maybe that's why he didn't look at me like other guys, and not for the reasons I'd created in my head. Maybe what I'd thought was heat was just...something else. Obviously something professional.

While he went into the kitchen to get us water bottles, I faced the windows, staring out at the lake. It was so smooth and peaceful. Serene.

When was the last time I took the time to notice nature? To feel true peace? To admire the natural beauty in the world around me?

Maybe I could use these next two weeks to commune with nature—or whatever people called it—instead of worrying about my stupid, clearly unrequited feelings for Wyatt. Maybe I could come up with some new songs. It's what I should be doing anyway—what I usually did when the world around me felt out of my control. Writing new songs always helped calm the chaos. Putting everything I was feeling on paper, creating a melody for it, helped me work through it all.

Maybe it was time to write about not only my unrequited feelings for Wyatt, but my true feelings about my ex, the media, my stalker. All the ways people constantly tried to make me feel like I wasn't good enough or was too much instead of realizing I was a human being with my own complex emotions about situations.

Yeah, that's what I'd do, my heart lifting slightly as a sense of purpose filled me. I'd focus on my job and leave Wyatt alone to do his.

And then my skin prickled with awareness, and heat at my back alerted me to Wyatt's body close to mine. His arm entered my field of vision, a water bottle firmly in his grasp that he offered to me. I took it, careful not to touch the rough fingers I'd fantasized about too many times.

"Thanks," I murmured.

He hummed, but didn't say anything else. The silence wrapped around us as we both stood there staring out at the turquoise lake.

I wasn't sure how much time passed before his low voice broke the silence. "You're not just a job. I...I care about your safety and well-being. More than I probably should."

My heart was in my throat, thumping so wildly I couldn't get words out even if I tried. But I couldn't stop the small smile that tugged on my lips as we continued to stand there, sipping our waters and letting the tension between us grow.

Rule #14

SHARING WON'T CROSS A LINE

Brynn

The next morning I came downstairs to find Wyatt sitting out on the patio. He'd moved the chair close to the door and had it open a crack, but he was facing out toward the lake. In his hands was a small chunk of wood and a pocketknife he was using to whittle.

I pulled the door open and stepped out, causing him to pause as he looked up at me. "Morning," I said, my voice still rough with sleep.

"Morning." I loved how rumbly and deep his voice was in the morning. It was my favorite part of having him with me all the time because I got to see all different sides of him.

"What are you working on?" I asked as I sat in the wooden Adirondack chair next to his.

He looked down at his hands like he'd forgotten he was holding something and then shook his head. "Nothing really."

I was disappointed, but I shouldn't have been. He was

paid to protect me, not to share his hobbies with me. I faced out toward the water, listening to the birds chirp in the early morning light and watching the gentle ripples in the water from fish coming up to the surface before immediately dropping back down.

"My grandpa taught me to whittle and carve wood when I was a kid." I faced Wyatt, surprised he was sharing with me. "We used to spend a week every summer with him. He wanted me to have a hobby I could do whenever I got bored, and he'd already taught my brother and me to always have a pocketknife on us. He figured anywhere we went we could find a stick or piece of wood. He taught me how to carve animals and then more elaborate things, and I guess it sort of stuck as a hobby. But he was right. Anywhere I went, even when I was a Seal, I could always find some wood and make something. It was a way to keep me grounded when my life felt chaotic." His lips tilted in a shy grin. "But it's also just fun to do sometimes."

"Will you teach me?"

His eyes widened as we stared at each other for a few seconds too long, but then he nodded and grabbed another small piece of wood next to him and handed it to me. He dug in his pocket for a second knife and I arched my brow. "Can never be too prepared," he said as his smile grew.

Was it possible for a heart to swoon? Because it felt like mine did. His smile was boyish and light. It was completely different from any look he'd ever given me, and it made me feel like I was getting to see a piece of him he rarely showed to others. Maybe I shouldn't have felt that way. I didn't know what he was like when he wasn't working, but it felt special, nonetheless.

He scooted closer and showed me how to properly hold the knife and to always carve away from my body—at least until I was more experienced. He talked me through the simple design, and I followed all his instructions with the same focus and care I would give to one of my songs. He didn't have to share this with me, and I didn't want him to think I wasn't taking it seriously.

By the time we were done, I'd made a small wooden heart. I beamed up at him, proud of myself. "I know it's simple, but I think it turned out pretty good for my first try." Sure, it wasn't perfect, but it was obviously a heart, and more than that, it was something Wyatt had taught me how to do, which made it even more special.

His smile was soft. "Sometimes the simplest designs mean the most."

Our gazes locked and his smile slipped away. My breaths grew uneven and my heart raced. He was so close, all it would take to kiss him would be to lean forward. His gaze dropped down to my mouth, and we both moved infinitesimally closer to each other. I could feel his breath skate across my face, and I was dying to know how he'd kiss me. Would he take over the kiss if I made the move first? Or would he savor it like a fine whiskey?

My eyelids started to close as I worked up the courage to close that small gap between us when he suddenly cleared his throat and sat back. His gaze was focused on the lake for a second before he stood up and shoved his now closed knife into his pocket.

"I'll make us some breakfast since I'm sure you're hungry." He didn't wait for my response before rushing inside.

I fell back against the Adirondack chair, my own gaze now lost to the gentle lapping of the lake from the soft morning breeze. I had been so close. So painfully close. And he'd once again reminded me with his actions that nothing could happen between us.

The problem was I'd seen the look in his eyes, recognized it for what it was. He wanted me as badly as I wanted him, and that knowledge was a dangerous thing to my crumbling resolve.

Rule #15

DON'T ATTEMPT TO SEDUCE YOUR BODYGUARD

Brynn

It only took two more days for my resolve to completely crumble. I really thought I had more self-restraint than that, but apparently all it took was a sexy, competent bodyguard to prove me wrong.

Everything he did turned me on.

Making dinner for us? Turned on.

Starting the fire in just a T-shirt and a pair of perfectly fitted jeans that sculpted his ass? Turned on.

And don't even get me started on watching this man chop wood. Jesus Christ. It should've been illegal to watch, it was so pornographic, especially when he took his shirt off.

I'd had to take an ice-cold shower and replay the moment in my mind afterward. Him running his forearm over his forehead to wipe off his sweat, then removing his shirt by grabbing the back of the neck and pulling it up over his head. The way it slowly revealed his six-pack abs and the V-lines that teased me as they disappeared into the band of his jeans. His thick biceps and veiny forearms. The way he tucked his shirt into the back pocket of his jeans and then grabbed the ax and lifted it into the air like it was nothing, simultaneously flexing every muscle in his arms and torso. I'm pretty sure I'd drooled, I was so mesmerized by his movements as I watched from the small window above the kitchen sink.

I needed another cold shower just thinking about it. Except tonight, I'd resolved to finally do something about these feelings Wyatt stirred up in me. I couldn't take this for another twelve days, and I was about ninety percent confident I wasn't alone in these feelings. His eyes lingered on me just a little longer than they should, his gaze more heated than was professional.

A nervous breath escaped me as I stared at myself in the mirror. I was wearing the sexiest thing I'd packed—a silk babydoll nightgown in a deep emerald green that complemented my fair complexion. It fell high on my thighs, but that was one of the things I'd loved about it because it showed off my long, toned legs. I wasn't wearing a bra, and my nipples were hard pebbles visible under the smooth silk. My hair fell in loose waves past my shoulders, and my face was free of makeup—something I'd noticed Wyatt seemed to like best since those were always the moments his gaze lingered the longest.

I stepped out of the bathroom where I'd been changing since we got to the cabin because the loft offered exactly zero privacy from the floor below. Wyatt was just finishing up the dishes from dinner, and he glanced over at me as he placed a glass on the shelf and closed the cupboard. The muscle in his jaw tightened and his dark eyes glided down my body with such fierce focus it made my core tighten and my inner thighs grow slick. No man had ever made me as wet as this man did with just one look.

Feeling emboldened by his stare, I stepped forward, closing the short distance between us in only four steps until my body was practically flush with his. I was out of practice when it came to seduction, and personally I preferred when the guy was the seducer. But I couldn't take the tension anymore, so I was putting myself out there and hoping Wyatt would catch me.

His Adam's apple bobbed in his throat as he swallowed, but otherwise, he didn't make a single move. I placed my hand on his shirt-covered abs which flexed immediately at my touch. Sliding my hand slowly up to his chest, then over his pecs, I tried to calm my staccato breathing. My heart raced as my gaze met his. "You feel this too, right?"

Okay, so not the sexiest thing I'd ever said. Clearly, I was *way* out of practice in the seduction department, but come on. Wasn't the guy supposed to see me in my barely there silk negligee and not be able to help himself? My heart sped up as he stood frozen like a statue. Why wasn't he ravishing me? Why wasn't he touching me or answering me?

Heat flooded my cheeks as embarrassment slammed into me like a semitruck going full speed into a rock wall.

Oh my God. What had I done? I almost choked on my own saliva as I tried to swallow.

"I'm s-sorry," I stammered as I stepped back, removing my hand from his body as if he'd burned me. And maybe he had because my whole body felt like it was being incinerated.

God, I'd just accosted my bodyguard. What the hell had I been thinking? Was I really so starved for affection and touch that I imagined everything between us? Maybe all those lingering stares were really just him doing his job and making sure I was fine.

I spun around, hoping he couldn't see how pink my cheeks had gotten with shame, but I only made it one step before his hand shot out and grabbed my arm, stopping me in my tracks. I couldn't bear to face him; there was no way he'd miss the humiliation setting my face on fire.

"Brynn," he growled my name and I dropped my head, accepting defeat.

I only hoped he'd keep his rejection short, so I could get up to the loft and bury myself under the comforter for the next twelve days. There was no way I'd be able to face him after this.

"I'm sorry," I said again, proud of myself for keeping my voice mostly composed. There was only the slightest quiver that gave away my shame. "I misread the situation. It won't happen again." Maybe if I reassured him before he could rip into me with how unprofessional my behavior was, we could skip the rest of this conversation and pretend this moment never happened.

My only saving grace at this point was that no one else was around to witness my embarrassment.

He spun me around, and before I could say another word, his firm lips were on mine. This was no sweet, tender kiss. It was rough, passionate, needy. He growled low in his throat as his other hand wrapped around my neck to hold me tight against him as his tongue slid across my lips. They parted on a gasp of surprise and he took full advantage, licking into my mouth and kissing me so thoroughly, I was sure my body would've melted into a puddle at his feet if he hadn't been holding me against him.

Rule #16

BE PROFESSIONAL AT ALL TIMES

Wyatt

I once thought this woman was going to be the death of me, but now I was wondering if she'd just be the death of my career.

Raf had one golden rule—don't fuck with clients. Only two guys had ever crossed that line as far as I knew, and both had been fired as soon as Raf found out—and Raf always found out.

But there was no way I could let her walk away with that hurt and ashamed look on her face thinking I didn't want her more than my next breath.

Because the truth was it had taken every ounce of restraint not to rip off that scrap of silk, lift her up, settle her on the counter, and dive between those long, smooth legs of hers to take the dessert I'd been dying to taste for weeks.

As it was, she already felt better than I'd imagined, and all she was doing was leaning against me as I slid my tongue inside her mouth, savoring the taste of her. She made a soft little mewling sound that had my body lighting up like the Fourth of fucking July.

A part of my brain screamed at me to stop. To rethink this. But the louder part told me I'd already sealed my fate. There was no going back now, so might as well take all that I wanted.

And I wanted it all.

I moved my hands down over her silk-covered body, loving the feel of her smooth skin against my rough palms and the way the fabric of her short nightgown bunched as I grabbed the hem and lifted it up her body one inch at a time. There was no way I was missing the unveiling of the body I'd dreamed about since that night I caught her hand between her legs in the bath, so I broke the kiss and pulled back just enough to see what I was doing.

Her heavy-lidded eyes stared at me with unrestrained want. Her lips were red and swollen from my kiss and her chest heaved, moving those perky tits up and down in the most tantalizing way.

"Is this mine?" I asked her, continuing to slowly pull her nightgown up.

Her lips parted and expelled a soft breath. "Do you want it to be?"

Ah, there she was. I liked this smart, confident woman much more than the hurt and ashamed woman she'd been when she thought I was rejecting her. I'd never stood a chance.

I pulled her silk nightgown off the rest of the way and dropped it to the floor without a second glance. My mouth watered as I traced the gentle curves of her tight body with my eyes, but I found my voice enough to respond to her.

"Maybe I should've been more clear. This *is mine.*" Then I wrapped one hand around the back of her neck and hauled her mouth to mine while my other hand slid over her firm breasts and down her toned stomach to the landing strip below. I slid one finger through her folds and let out a low groan at how wet she was already.

She gasped into my mouth as I slid my soaked finger inside, feeling her pussy tighten around my digit. Fuck, she was tight. It would be a snug fit, but I had plenty of time to ready her for my cock. Doing what I'd imagined earlier, I pulled my hand away, grabbed her hips, and set her on the edge of the counter.

"Wha—"

I placed my wet finger against her lips, silencing her instantly. Her eyes heated as her tongue darted out, but I pulled my finger away and sucked it into my mouth instead, my gaze never leaving hers.

"That's my dessert, not yours. You'll get yours in a minute."

I closed my eyes in bliss as her tangy taste burst across my tongue. Fuck, I was going to be addicted to this flavor, I could already tell.

Opening my eyes, I focused on her. I pushed her thighs wider apart and then got down on my knees to worship her the way she deserved to be worshipped every day. Her fingers slid into my thick hair as I licked up her seam to her swollen clit.

"Oh fuck," she whispered, her legs already tightening around my head.

I had half a mind to ask her when the last time was she'd been eaten out, but the thought of another man between her perfect legs only pissed me off. Brynn was mine now, and I'd wipe the memory of any other man out of her mind completely.

For her, there would be no one else. No one who made

her feel pleasure. No one who could make her come as hard as I could.

No one but me.

I licked inside her drenched pussy, coating my mouth in her cream, loving the way she arched her back and pressed her body closer to my mouth.

"Wyatt," she moaned, just like the night she'd been in the bathtub.

"Mmm," I hummed against her pussy, causing her thighs to tremble from the added vibration.

"You're going to come on my tongue and let me lick you clean," I told her.

Her breathing was ragged, her eyes glazed with lust and her chest pink from the pleasure she'd already felt, but she had no idea how good it was about to get.

Without breaking our gaze, I slid one finger, then two, moving them in a V shape inside her to stretch her out so she could take my cock when she was ready. Her cheeks grew even more pink, but she didn't close her eyes. She held her body mostly still, apart from the small quiver of her stomach and thighs that gave away how hard she was working to remain still.

I flicked my thumb over her plump clit, eliciting a sharp inhale from her. "Look at how this pretty pussy weeps for me." At my words, she grew slicker, and I couldn't fight the groan that escaped.

My cock had never been so hard as it was right then, but there was no way I was going to touch it when my hands had better things to touch, like her perfect glistening pussy and her beaded nipples that were just crying out for attention.

Standing up, I took one needy nipple into my mouth and sucked it the way I planned to suck her clit. Brynn's head tilted back as she let out another sexy moan, and her fingers curled around my neck, holding me against her body. I pumped my fingers inside her tight pussy while I continued to lick and suck her nipples until she was a mewling mess on the counter.

"Wyatt, please."

"Please what, baby?"

"Make me come," she pleaded. "I'm so c-close."

I could feel how close she was, her pussy fluttering against my fingers. I pushed a third inside and curled them on the slide out, then repeated that movement as I got back on my knees to suck her clit. All it took was one more thrust and she exploded, her flavor flooding my fingers and my mouth as I licked her clean, just like I'd promised.

When I'd licked every drop, I stood back up and pulled off my shirt over my head, dropping it onto the floor next to her nightgown. Her pupils were dilated as she traced down my abs and then back up to meet my gaze. I held her stare as I unbuckled my belt, undid the button and zipper on my jeans, and then pushed them down my legs with my boxer briefs. I was already barefoot, so I pulled my feet through and then kicked the clothing aside. Her pink tongue darted out to slide across her bottom lip as she looked hungrily at my erection.

Gripping it in my fist, I gave it a tug, rolling over the head to use the precum there as light lubrication.

"You ready for this?" I asked her.

Her gaze shot to mine. "There's no going back now."

I shook my head. "There wasn't any going back the second my lips touched yours. This just solidifies that you're now mine completely."

"I think I was yours even before you kissed me," she whispered.

A moment passed between us, the air shifting around us, thickening into something deeper, more meaningful.

She was mine, but maybe more importantly, I was hers. I'd been so focused on making her forget every other man that came before me and yet here I was, not able to think of a single woman in existence who wasn't her.

I stepped forward, ready to slide inside her—already knowing she'd feel better than anything I'd ever felt before —when I stopped and reality came crashing down on me.

"Fuck," I muttered, dropping my head to hers.

"What?" she asked.

"I don't have a condom." Why would I? I hadn't planned for this. I sure as hell wasn't going to prepare for something that I told myself I would never allow to happen.

And then her sweet, soft voice broke the quiet. "I tested negative on my last health check after my ex and I broke up, and I'm on birth control."

I lifted my head, fixating on her face and the earnest expression there.

She ran a delicate finger over the fine hair on my chest. "If you've been tested and are clear, then we could still do this, if you want."

If I wanted? Was she serious right now? What man wouldn't want to be buried balls deep and bare inside her?

Without even bothering to answer her with words, I notched my cock against her slick pussy and pushed inside slowly.

"Fuck, baby. You're so goddamn tight."

She gripped my waist, holding me against her. "Don't stop," she pleaded.

"Fuck no, I'm not stopping." I dropped my forehead back to hers and watched where we were connected intimately. "You're too tempting."

She huffed out a laugh that turned into a moan as I buried myself to the hilt inside her. I held still, afraid if I moved too soon I might actually come. It had been a long time, and she felt so insanely good that it took more brain power than I'd ever used during sex to make sure this wasn't embarrassingly short.

She cupped my face and brought my lips to hers. The kiss was soft, delicate, more intimate than what we were already doing with our bodies. When she pulled back, she stared at me, her green eyes speaking volumes I didn't think she'd ever voice.

She was scared I was going to hurt her—not physically, as she had to know I'd cut my own arms off before I ever hurt her physically, but emotionally. That I might break her heart.

And the thought that she might give me her heart—that I could be worthy of such a thing—took me to another level. I pulled out and thrust back inside her body, harder, needier, hungrier for her than I knew was possible. I surged forward and took her lips in a bruising kiss, sliding my tongue against hers when she parted her lips for me and thrusting my hips forward at the same time. Without any warning, her pussy convulsed against mine, and she scratched my back as her orgasm hit her full force and pulled mine out of me at the same time.

A shiver slid down my back as pleasure wreaked havoc with my mind. Sex was supposed to feel good, but fuck me, it had never felt *that* good.

I couldn't bear the idea of pulling out of her so soon, so I stayed buried inside her and instead broke our kiss so I could look into her eyes and check on her. A flush spread from her cheeks down to her chest. She was panting, breathless, but her eyes were shining and her lips were tilted up in a smile.

"You've gone and done it now," I told her.

"Done what?" she asked playfully before dropping a peck to my lips.

"Made me addicted to you," I said as I pulled her off the counter, my still mostly hard dick inside her, and carried her out of the kitchen toward the loft.

I had plans for the rest of the night, and the counter wasn't going to cut it.

Rule #17

DON'T HAVE THE BEST SEX OF YOUR LIFE WITH YOUR BODYGUARD

Brynn

My thighs were still shaking from the intensity of my last two orgasms as he carried me up the stairs to the loft. I peppered kisses on his face and then down his neck, and his last step at the top of the stairs almost faltered. I could only tell by the way his arms banded tighter around me to secure me in his grasp for the split second it took for him to steady himself.

He set me on the bed and caged me in with his arms by my shoulders. His mouth met mine, and he slid that skilled tongue of his across my lips as if he was seeking entry.

I'd give him anything he wanted if he kept making me feel this good.

His lips kissed across my jawline to my neck where he sucked on an especially tender spot, and I let out a moan as my core tightened with need.

I slid my fingers into his thick hair, gripping the strands tight enough that he growled against my neck.

"You keep that up and I'll fuck you into next week."

"Don't threaten me with a good time," I moaned as he sucked harder on that spot, no doubt leaving a hickey behind.

The thought of this man marking me as his had arousal pooling between my thighs once again.

He lifted his hard, fit body up and stared down at me, his pupils blown wide from desire. "Fuck, you're perfect for me."

I swallowed thickly, not sure what to say to that. Honestly, I was afraid if I opened my mouth I'd confess that this man already had my heart in knots.

He kissed down my chest until he reached the stiff peaks of my nipples and took one in his mouth. I tilted my head back and sucked in a sharp breath. "Wyatt."

"That's right, baby. Say my name while I make you come again."

He continued his path south, his tongue darting out and tasting my skin as he moved closer and closer to where I was already soaked for him.

"Fuck, look at this pretty pussy. So fucking wet and ready for me."

I picked my head up to watch him dart his tongue out and close his eyes as he let out a deep groan. When he opened them, they met mine, and the hunger there made me forget to breathe. He broke our gaze to stare at my pussy as he ate me out like a starving man. He slid his tongue through my folds, then nibbled lightly up toward my mound where he once again swirled that talented tongue around my clit. It was pleasurable, but not enough to get me off.

And then he added his fingers. It was like he had a roadmap directly to my pleasure spots, and he hit multiple at once as he sucked my clit into his mouth repeatedly while rubbing on a spot inside me that had stars bursting across my vision. My thighs tightened around his head, trembling from the intensity of my release as a scream ripped from my throat.

My whole body was shaking as I came down from the most intense orgasm I'd ever had. When I gathered the strength to open my eyes and became aware of my surroundings again, I found Wyatt with a smug grin on his face as he stayed perched between my thighs, kissing them gently. His mouth was still wet from my release, and there was something sexy and naughty about it that pulled at my needy core.

He kissed up my body until he took my lips in another soul-searing kiss. While he was kissing me senseless, he nudged us up the bed so we were fully on it instead of half off like I had been. Without breaking the kiss, he thrust deep inside me. I sucked in a sharp breath, inhaling his air.

"Oh God."

"You can just call me Wyatt," he said with a smile in his voice.

I slapped at his back, but then he changed his angle, and what had started as a slap ended with me sliding my nails down his back as the pleasure threatened to drag me under.

"Fuck yes. Scratch me and leave your mark on me," he groaned, kissing my neck where I was sure he'd left a hickey.

I scratched down his back again and went down as far as I could reach. He lifted his head, his neck stretching out like the sensation of him fucking me combined with my nails scratching down his back had him right on the edge.

When he turned his gaze on me, his eyes were dark and possessive. "You ready to go for a ride?" he asked, his voice husky.

My brows furrowed, and I was about to ask him what

the hell he was talking about when he flipped us so I was straddling him. We both let out a shuddering gasp as he impaled me so deep, I swore I could feel him in my belly.

"Oh fuck," I cried.

"Ride me, Brynn. Show me who I belong to."

That was a challenge I had no intention of backing down from. Bracing my hands on his toned chest, I found a rhythm that had both of us moaning.

His hands gripped my hips, and he pulled me down hard onto his dick, holding me tight against his body. "Rock those sexy hips. Make yourself come on my cock."

I slid forward and tilted my head back at the sensation of my clit rubbing against his hard abs, while his thick cock stretched my pussy more than I'd ever experienced.

Picking up my pace, I followed his instructions. "That's it," he grunted. "Rub that needy little clit all over me. Cover me with your come."

My muscles tensed from how close I was, and I let out a whimper as I teetered right on the edge. Then his hands on my hips tightened and he took over the motion, moving me back and forth faster than I had been until the pleasure reached a fever pitch. I scraped my nails down his chest as I cried out his name.

"That's a good girl, coming all over my cock. Fucking hell, you squeeze me so good when you come." He thrust up into me, and the aftershocks of my orgasm made my whole body tremble and shake.

"Wyatt, please."

"Please what, baby?"

I wasn't entirely sure. My head was so cloudy from all the orgasms.

My clit still throbbed, and if he kept thrusting and hitting that spot deep inside, I was pretty sure he could make me come again, but I also wasn't sure I would survive another orgasm. My body couldn't stop shaking from the intensity I'd already experienced.

He sat up, holding me so my chest was pressed against his. "You want me to make that pretty pussy come again?"

I nodded.

"I need you to say the words, Brynn."

"Yes," I pleaded. "Show me who I belong to," I whispered, repeating his words and feeling insanely vulnerable.

His eyes burned into me, causing heat to fill my stomach and my chest in a way that only added to the pleasure. He made me feel like I really did belong to him. Like I had found my person at last and I'd never feel alone again.

Wyatt was the antidote to my loneliness. He was my reward for the hard journey I'd already experienced. I never wanted to leave this moment or lose this feeling.

He rolled us over so he was hovering over me and gripped the back of my neck as he thrust inside me, hitting that spot only he'd ever found over and over again. I wrapped my legs around his hips and locked my ankles on his back, meeting each of his thrusts until we were both moaning and grunting from the exertion.

He stared at me like he could see into my soul and didn't break the contact, even as he slid his hand between us and rubbed my clit until my orgasm ripped through me. My pussy tightened on his cock and with one last thrust, he came with me, shouting my name before burying his face in my neck.

Holy shit.

I was pretty sure Wyatt had ruined me for anyone else.

Rule #18

A REAL RELATIONSHIP CAN'T START WITH SEX

Brynn

Wyatt's lips traced my collarbone as he slid a finger inside my pussy. Another moan escaped me as my body felt new levels of pleasure.

It had never been this way before—so good, so addicting, so orgasmic.

Wyatt had promised that he'd make me come on his tongue, fingers, and cock, and he'd delivered on all three, several times over. And yet, I still craved the feel of his body inside and on top of mine. I wanted his touch at all hours of the day.

For three days, we'd done nothing but have sex and occasionally remember to eat. But even when we were eating, we were touching each other. I wasn't sure how I was ever going to survive without his touch once we left the happy little bubble of this cabin.

But that was a worry for another day.

I sank my fingers into his mussed-up hair as his lips moved down, over my breasts, before he took one nipple between his teeth. He peeked up at me as he tugged, the corners of his lips pulling up into a cheeky grin. At the same time, he rocked his hips, canting his steel erection so it slid along my wet and swollen pussy lips. Using one of his hands, he grabbed the base of his cock and notched the head at my entrance, watching our bodies join slowly until he was seated deep.

"God, I'll never get tired of watching your body take my cock."

His mouth was dirtier than anyone I'd ever met, and I'd had no idea that dirty talk was such a turn-on for me. I loved hearing the words that came out of his mouth, the dirty demands, the way he'd call me his. All of it was a seduction I'd never experienced and, like everything else about him, had grown addicted to.

I slid a hand down to rub my clit as he pumped inside me, but I'd only barely touched it when he grabbed my hand and pulled my finger up to his mouth. He sucked it between his lips, his tongue swirling over the pad and licking away even the tiniest trace of my arousal. All the while, his hips still thrust forward and back, teasing me closer to my next orgasm.

"Wyatt..."

"Yeah, baby, say my name just like that while I fuck another orgasm out of this perfect body."

His words took me right to the edge of release, and then he dropped his hand to rub his thumb over my clit just the way he knew I needed. I fell over the cliff, my orgasm arcing through me and making my thighs shake where they rested against Wyatt's hips.

He pumped three more times and followed me off the edge, bending over to kiss my lips as he came inside me.

We lay there for a few minutes, my fingers tracing invisible lines on his body, the sweat cooling on our skin before either of us spoke.

"How sore are you?" he asked.

"I'm okay," I said, although I was definitely more swollen down there than I'd ever been. I'd never had a sex fest before, but there was no other name for the amount of sex we'd had in the last few days.

His hand cupped the front of my neck, his thumb pushing up under my chin so I was forced to look into his discerning gaze. "Tell me the truth, not some lie because you think you'll be a burden if you're honest."

I swallowed thickly. It was like he could see my soul and there was no way I could ever hide from him again.

"I was already a little sore from last night's activities. I'll probably feel more sore once you pull out."

His eyes darted back and forth between mine, probably searching to make sure that was the truth. It was. He pressed his lips against my forehead, making my heart squeeze tightly in my chest at the tenderness.

"I'm sorry. I should've given you more time to recover."

I wrapped my arms around his waist to his back. "I wasn't complaining. Everything still felt good."

He shook his head at me, the left corner of his lips curving up in a small smile. "You never complain. About anything. Even when you see someone doing something wrong, you redirect them in the most polite and positive way I've ever witnessed." He brushed a strand of loose hair away from my face. "You're always taking care of everyone's feelings and making sure things run smoothly. But who takes care of you?"

A lump formed in my throat. "No one," I choked out. It was true. Grant used to when I was underage, but since I'd turned eighteen, I'd taken on every aspect of my business. I delegated, sure, but everything was still my responsibility because I was the boss.

His gaze turned fierce. "Not anymore. Now you've got me, okay?"

"Only until I stop paying you." It wasn't often my pessimistic side came out to play, but unfortunately, I couldn't trust that this was real. As much as I wanted to, and as much as I planned to enjoy every single second alone with Wyatt, I couldn't deny that I knew it would all end once we left this cabin. He'd never choose us over a job he was so good at. And I'd never ask him to either.

He frowned down at me and shook his head. "If you haven't realized all that I've already given up for you, then I clearly have more work to do. The second I kissed you, that was it. I'm yours, no payment required. If you hadn't noticed, I'm not interested in your money or your fame."

I parted my lips to respond, but he placed one finger against them. "Let's go take a bath. The hot water will help with the soreness."

He didn't wait for me to respond. Instead he got out of the bed, picked me up, and carried me down to the bathroom, placing me on the vanity while he got the water running in the big claw-foot tub. He walked the short distance over to me, spread my legs wide and then ducked down, but instead of licking me or doing something equally naughty like I expected, he smiled up at me and opened the door under the sink.

"Had to grab the Epsom salts," he said, chuckling. "What did you think I was going to do, naughty girl?"

My cheeks heated and his chuckle turned into a full laugh. When Wyatt laughed, he looked younger and, if possible, sexier. I loved seeing him laugh. He dropped a kiss to my mouth before he turned around and sprinkled some Epsom salts into the bath.

"How'd you know those were under the sink?"

Without looking back at me he said, "I took stock of everything the first night we were here, while you were asleep."

That definitely sounded like something he'd do. He dipped his hand in the water and must've found it up to his standards because he walked over to me, slid his hands under my ass, and lifted me up into his arms before carrying me back to the now full tub.

He set me on my feet, but held my hand and helped me in. He turned like he was going to leave, but I grabbed his arm. "You're coming in too, right?"

He glanced down at the tub. "It'll be a snug fit."

My lips lifted easily in a wide smile. "That's what she said."

He huffed out a chuckle, shaking his head at my ridiculousness, and then gestured for me to move forward. It took a little finagling since he was so tall, but we both managed to fit. I couldn't deny I loved being snuggled up to him in the warm water.

He grabbed the washcloth hanging off the side and dipped it into the water before running it over my chest and arms.

"Did you always want to be a bodyguard?" I asked him.

"Not particularly. I wanted to be a firefighter when I was little and then I joined the navy right out of high school and went the special forces route. That's how I met Raf— Rafferty Carmichael. We were in the same unit for most of our time in the service, but he got out a few years before I did and set up Carmichael Security. By the time my contract was about to be up, he had things up and running and offered me a job with better pay and benefits. Plus I could be close to home, which was nice because I missed seeing my brother regularly. It was one of those things I just happened to be good at, and it fell into my lap."

One thing I loved most about Wyatt was that he shared information so freely with me. I'd dated guys before where getting information out of them was like pulling teeth, but not with Wyatt. A simple question and he gave me a full and complete answer. But it also just made me want to know more about him.

"What would you do if you weren't a bodyguard?"

His hand stilled briefly before he continued washing my body. "I'm not really sure."

A sliver of guilt wormed its way into my conscience. I was costing him his job. If he meant what he said when he implied he'd already given things up for me, then being with me was going to cost him more than it would cost me. It didn't feel fair, and I worried that he might come to resent me later because of it.

"Maybe you could do something with your hands. Like wood carving or something."

He kissed the back of my head. "That's not a bad idea. Did you always want to be a performer?"

I appreciated that he didn't call me a pop star like most people did. "Yeah, pretty much. I've been singing since I was little and started writing my own songs in middle school. My parents weren't performers, but they had high profile jobs and were always schmoozing with actors, singers, producers, agents. It was probably part nepotism, part right place, right time that got me my start. But once I started releasing music and performing for larger and larger crowds, I knew there was nothing else I wanted to do."

"Is there anything you wish you could change about it?"

"About being famous?"

He placed a kiss on my neck. "Yeah."

"I don't know. Sometimes I think it would be nice to have more privacy, more genuine friendships and relationships. Most of the people I'm closest to are on my payroll, and I can't help but think they only care about me *because* I pay them."

By the way his body stiffened behind me, he knew that he fell in that category too, even if I wished he didn't.

"I think I accepted a long time ago that what I was sacrificing was worth it. There was a moment about three years ago when I almost quit. I was so exhausted from being in the limelight all the time. I'd gone out in public and been a little bloated, and the tabloids went wild saying I was pregnant with my music producer's baby, which was insane and completely untrue, but the story was near impossible to kill because people eat up that kind of crap. I was going to quietly disappear and then I ran into a fan when I went out to buy groceries. I'll never forget her for as long as I live. She started crying and told me how my music saved her. Literally saved her. She was going to commit suicide after a particularly rough patch in her life. I had just released my single "Stronger Than," and she heard it on the radio right before she was about to down a bottle of pills. She told me how she sobbed as she listened to every word and then played it on repeat for several hours before she called a friend for help. That song was already a year old by the time we ran into each other, and she'd completely turned her life around. All because *my* song played on the radio at the right time.

"It was the first time I really accepted that I did my job for my fans and not just for myself. There is some catharsis when I write my songs because I can write about my personal experiences in a way that's relatable to others, so it's not like I *only* do it for my fans. But they're a big factor in what keeps me going when things get hard."

I swirled my hand beneath the water, getting lost in the ripples I made. "Sometimes I feel guilty for feeling so lonely when I'm privileged beyond belief. I have a life so many people dream about, and it makes me feel ungrateful during those times when I wish I had something..."

"Something real?" he finished for me.

My chest squeezed painfully, and emotions thickened my voice when I spoke. "Yeah."

He wrapped his hand around mine. His was so much larger than mine and yet somehow they fit together perfectly. "This is the realest thing I've felt in a very long time," he said, his voice low, but every word crystal clear.

"Me too," I confessed. And that's what scared me so much.

Rule #19

DON'T TOUCH YOURSELF IN FRONT OF SOMEONE ELSE

Brynn

I slapped my winning hand down on the blanket we were sitting on in front of the roaring fire and raised my hands up in the air. "Aha, gotcha. Finally!"

Wyatt was a skilled poker player, something I'd learned by losing over and over again. But after ten rounds, I had finally gotten a good hand that I *knew* there was no way he could beat.

His lips tilted in a sexy smile that had my insides turning to mush, and his heated gaze watched me like he was thinking about devouring me. My smile faltered and my shoulders sagged.

"No way. You did not beat me," I said, disappointment bringing me down from the high of what I thought had been an obvious victory.

He looked down at his cards and then tossed them face down into the pile before scooping up all the cards. "Nope, I didn't. Another round?" he asked, already shuffling the deck.

I placed my hand on his, staring at him intently. "I won? For real?"

He smiled, his eyes softening as he stared at me. "Yeah, baby. You did."

I jumped up and did a happy dance on the blanket, causing Wyatt to burst out in laughter, but I was too happy to be self-conscious. "I knew it! I knew it was a good hand!"

He tossed the cards to the side and stood up, wrapping his arms around my waist and pulling me against his chest. I laughed, happier than I'd been in so long. I felt lighter too. Not from winning the game, but from the last several days of toe-curling sex, great company, and a lot of laughter from the simplest things.

Wyatt slid his hand through my hair, which looked redder in the firelight, before moving it to the nape of my neck, while his other hand held me around the waist. I was so lost in the warmth of his gaze I didn't even realize right away that he was swaying us, as if we were dancing to a slow song only the two of us could hear.

My chest tightened the longer I stared in his eyes, losing myself in his gaze. "Wyatt," I whispered, not sure if it was meant to be a plea or a question.

The corner of his mouth tilted up. "Dance with me."

"There's no music."

"Sing for me."

"What?"

His thumb brushed the lobe of my ear. "You heard me."

It had been a long time since I'd sung in front of someone without instruments and costumes. I was stripped down to just my voice. I nibbled my lip for a minute before I decided to sing the song I'd started writing over the past week.

"All eyes on me,
I can hardly breathe.
Whispers in my head and every corner of the
*   street*
All the things unsaid to people I'll never
*   meet.*
I cry, I plead, I beg,
But only in my head.
Everyone wants to hear what I have to say,
But no one wants to listen to the words.
Like a statue in a museum, I stand tall and
*   frozen*
Surrounded by prying eyes, but still all
*   alone.*
And then came you
Like a beacon in the darkness
A light who saw through
All the chaos and loneliness
And now all I see is you.
All I see is you."

His eyes burned into mine as I dropped the final note. "It's a little rough. It's a new song I've been working on." I swallowed thickly as he continued to not say anything. I dropped my gaze. "I know it's not very—"

He tilted my chin up, forcing me to look at him. "I loved it. Every word." His tone held such sincerity, I had no reason to doubt him.

He leaned forward, pressing his lips against mine in a kiss that was softer, more tender, than any we'd shared before. There was so much care, so much emotion behind it, tears burned my eyes.

He broke the kiss but rested his forehead against mine.

"I think I could listen to you sing my grocery list and think it was worthy of a Grammy. You have such a beautiful voice, Brynn."

"Thank you," I said, my voice hoarse from all the emotions bubbling under the surface that I was holding back.

It was too soon to feel all the things this man brought out in me.

He kissed me again, his tongue skimming across my lips until I parted them and he could slide it into my mouth. Our kiss grew heated like it always seemed to whenever our mouths met. I grabbed the hem of his shirt and ripped it off, my fingers gliding over his firm pecs and toned abs.

"God, you have the hottest body."

He laughed. "You stole the words right out of my mouth," he said, but his gaze was clearly locked on where my breasts were straining against his T-shirt that I'd thrown on before we started playing poker.

Following my lead, he gripped the hem of the shirt and pulled it slowly off my body. He tossed it onto the floor toward the couch without breaking his gaze from mine. He swallowed hard, and I watched in fascination as his Adam's apple bobbed. It still amazed me that he seemed to be as affected by me as I was by him.

It felt like a miracle that life had brought us together.

He closed the distance between us with one step, wrapping my hair around his hand and tilting my head back as he sealed his lips over mine in a kiss that I felt down to my toes. His other hand slid down my body, gently pinching my peaked nipples before moving down to my clit. I let out a whimpering mewl when he only brushed over it once and then squealed when he picked me up and kneeled, gently laying me down beneath him.

He sat back on his heels and stared at my body like it was a feast made just for him. When his gaze met mine, there was a challenge there that had my interest piqued.

"I want to watch while you touch yourself."

My mouth parted in an O. "W-what?"

"I haven't been able to stop thinking about you masturbating in that bathtub and everything the bubbles covered. I want to see it. I want to see the way you bring yourself pleasure."

He brought me more pleasure than I'd ever felt on my own, but I wouldn't deny his request. Truth was I hadn't stopped thinking about it either. And masturbating—at least on purpose—in front of someone was something I'd never done. I wanted to experience everything with him.

I moved my hand to my clit, but he gripped my wrist and arched a brow. "Do you always just go for the gold?"

"No, but I thought that's what you wanted to see."

He leaned over me, his face just an inch from mine. "Touch yourself the way I would touch you. The way I would tease you until you were so wet it dripped down to the blanket. The way I would bring you right to the edge before launching you over. Can you do that, baby?"

I wasn't sure I could even breathe from how turned on he'd just made me. "Yes," I whispered. A part of me wanted to beg him to just do it himself and do exactly what he'd said, but the bigger part of me wanted to prove to him I could do this.

Despite the fact I knew he'd already seen me do this before, I was surprised by how self-conscious I suddenly felt. I wasn't typically a woman who lacked confidence, but even when I had in the past, I'd lived by the mantra "fake it 'til you make it."

So, I did exactly what he'd told me to do. I pretended

my hand was his hand. It wasn't as callused, so I closed my eyes to try to really get into it.

"Look at me when you touch yourself."

My eyes snapped open and I met his hungry gaze. My heart rate spiked, but so did the arousal between my legs. Not breaking eye contact with him, I slid my hand down my chest to my breasts. I swirled my finger around my nipple, but it didn't feel as good as it did when he sucked on it, which gave me an idea. Sticking two fingers in my mouth, I sucked on them once and then licked them thoroughly making sure they were nice and wet. A low growl escaped from Wyatt and in my periphery, he flexed his fingers where they rested on his thighs.

I took my wet fingers and slid them over my breast, then formed a V with my first two fingers and rubbed them on either side of my hard nipple, occasionally pinching the nipple between them like Wyatt so often did with his teeth —not enough to hurt, but enough to send a shot of lust straight to my pussy.

I rubbed my thighs together, hoping to ease the slight ache since I knew Wyatt expected me to play with myself longer before I moved down to my clit.

His gaze dropped to my pussy where I had no doubt he could see how wet I was.

"Already?" he asked, his voice hoarse.

"Just thinking about you turns me on, Wyatt. Touching myself while imagining it's you and seeing how badly you want me is enough to make me combust from need."

He closed his eyes and his jaw clenched as if he was in pain, but when he opened his eyes, it wasn't pain there. It was desire. The fiercest desire I'd ever seen.

"I need to touch my clit."

"Do it," he growled, granting me the permission I'd been hoping for.

I slid my hand down my toned stomach to my plump clit and rubbed it softly. My fingers had gotten dry from when I played with my nipples, and I thought about dipping them in the arousal that was pooling barely an inch away from my clit, but I loved the fire in Wyatt's eyes so much when I'd sucked them in my mouth that I decided to do it again. Except as soon as I got close to my mouth, Wyatt grabbed my wrist and brought my fingers to his mouth instead.

It was my turn to wear a hungry expression, because watching Wyatt suck on my fingers and lick them was insanely erotic in a way I never thought it would be.

Once he got them good and wet, he placed my fingers directly on my clit, and then put his hands back on his thighs, gripping them tight as he watched me like he was right on the cliff's edge from pouncing on me and taking over.

I swirled my clit with my now wet fingers, getting more turned on with every second that I had Wyatt's attention on my every move. My pussy was clenching on nothing, the pleasure building and building and building. My chest heaved as my breath started to come out in heavy pants, my eyelids lowered as it became harder and harder to keep them open once the pleasure grew to a crescendo.

"Wyatt," I moaned. "I'm gonna come."

"Come for me, baby. Let me see you."

I rubbed faster, maintaining the same pressure but increasing the pace until I couldn't keep my eyes open anymore and stars burst across my vision. I cried out, my legs shaking as my orgasm rolled through me like a lazy, yet powerful wave.

I dropped my head back to the blanket, my body spent and my chest heaving. God, that was a heady experience.

A wet tongue slid through my folds, and I lifted my head to find Wyatt's face between my legs, his tongue licking up my wet slit to my still sensitive clit. My body shook as each lick elicited a new tremor.

"Fuck, you taste so good," he groaned. "I never want to stop touching you, tasting you, making you mine."

"Don't stop," I choked out, pleasure already building again.

I didn't want him to ever stop.

Because it didn't matter if it was too soon—I couldn't deny that I was falling for this man so hard. And as he brought me to another earth-shattering orgasm, I thought of all the ways he made me feel and then a revelation hit me harder than the concern that I was falling in love with him.

"Did you really win that hand earlier?"

He laughed hard before kissing me gently, winking at me, and then pulling me up into his arms and carrying me up to the loft.

Rule #20

DON'T PLAN TOO FAR INTO THE FUTURE

Wyatt

Her bare skin was so smooth under my rough fingertips as I traced lines across her back and the arm that was draped over my waist. I'd never been a fan of snuggling when I slept, but with Brynn the idea of not touching her was painful.

We'd had sex well into the early morning and I didn't want to wake her, but I also couldn't sleep any longer either. My time as a Seal had beat that ability out of me. I could function decently on three hours of sleep, although normally I aimed for four or five. I glanced at the clock that was on the nightstand and figured I'd gotten about three and a half before my body decided that was enough and woke me up. So now I was just staring at the woman who'd ensnared me completely.

She was so much more than I'd thought she'd be. Before we'd come to the cabin, I'd been attracted to how her mind worked from a business standpoint and the way she treated those around her. Now that I'd spent so much uninterrupted time with her hidden away in our own private cabin in the woods, I was learning new things about her that had skyrocketed that attraction into something so much more.

She loved to read, although I hadn't given her much time to do so because I couldn't stop touching her, which inevitably led to us having sex. She also tended to stare out the window and hum quietly to herself. I hadn't quite figured out if it was something she did to soothe herself or if she was coming up with songs. Knowing what I knew now, I wouldn't be surprised if it was a combo—making music soothed her soul, even if it also added a shitload of chaos to her life. She'd told me her fans were the reason she still wrote songs and sang at all, but I wasn't sure she even realized how much she lit up when she was writing down lyrics in the notebook she kept with her or when her humming turned into a tune she liked and her smile lifted her face.

I'd teased my brother for falling in love with Sadie in such a short amount of time, but I understood how it had happened now. I could no longer deny that what I was feeling for Brynn had far exceeded anything I'd ever felt before. I was risking it all to be with her, and it was a risk I would happily take over and over again without question.

She stirred and nuzzled into my chest. "What time is it?"

"Early. Go back to sleep," I murmured.

She kissed my chest before adjusting so she was resting her head on my shoulder and able to look at me. "Couldn't sleep?"

I shook my head. "Old military habits die hard."

She slid her hand over my chest, the touch both soothing something inside me I hadn't realized was unsettled and turning me on like no one else ever had.

"What made you join the military?"

I stared up at the ceiling thinking about how I'd been at eighteen. "My parents raised us boys to be fiercely independent, not necessarily on purpose. But as much as I was good at school, I didn't enjoy it, so college didn't look that appealing. I wasn't really sure what field I wanted to go into, but I loved doing physical work. A high school buddy was joining the army, so I looked into it and decided I wanted to join the navy because I preferred being close to the water."

"Why don't you think your parents meant for you to be so independent?"

I let out a deep sigh as I tried to find the words to explain my family. "My parents are good people. They loved my brother and me, but they were always so busy with their own things that we often got left to handle everything at home by ourselves. My dad was a salesman so he was gone a lot, and our mom ran her own business that was fairly successful, but not successful enough that she could have a lot of employees, which meant she worked a lot. Most of the time it was just me and my brother, and we learned pretty quickly how to take care of ourselves. We're no worse for wear because of our upbringing. We still talk to our folks. We just don't have that close of a relationship with them. My brother's always been the person I went to whenever I needed advice or anything."

"That's how it is for me with Grant." She rubbed her finger in a circle on my pec, looking lost in thought for a minute before she spoke again. "My parents wanted to be celebrities. They would never admit that, but it's true. They were always going to Hollywood parties and trying to become friends with bigwigs in the entertainment industry. The first time I sang was in front of all their friends. I'd only learned to play guitar because I thought if I could perform for their friends maybe they'd be proud of me and spend more time with me. They didn't. I performed. Their friends oohed and aahed and then my parents sent me to bed so they could keep partying. I remember going to my room and crying because I felt like nothing I did would be good enough for them. Grant came into my room and held me until the tears finally stopped. He told me they didn't understand how special I was and that was on them, not me. He was my biggest cheerleader, and when I started getting booked for gigs, he was the one that took me. I didn't even tell my parents because at that point I was afraid they'd only show up to see who they could rub elbows with. It wasn't until I got really popular that they finally found out."

"And let me guess... they wanted to show you off?"

Her lips tilted up into a smile, but it didn't reach her eyes. "You would be right."

"Do you talk to them now?"

"No. I cut them off when I turned eighteen. Grant did too."

"I'm glad you have him." The thought of her not having anyone in her corner made my chest ache.

When she smiled this time, her eyes lit up. "Me too. He's only a few years older than I am, but I used to tease him all the time for being my dad because truthfully he kind of was. I don't know what I would've done without him."

"Now you've got me too," I murmured against her hair as I dropped a kiss there. I never wanted her to feel like she was alone again. As far as I was concerned, I would have her back until my dying breath.

I was already picturing our future too clearly. Her in a white dress, a honeymoon somewhere tropical, her stomach rounded with our children, her as a mom. I bet she'd be amazing—her heart was too big to be anything but an incredible mother. I could already picture family vacations, long nights with sick kids, watching our kids play sports or perform like their mom. For the first time in my life, I could see it all with complete clarity. And every bit of it felt right. It felt like this was where I was always meant to be, right here, holding this incredible woman in my arms and preparing to spend the rest of my life loving her with everything I had.

She pulled back enough so she could look me in the eye. "Do I have you?" Her words came out in a whisper, as if she was afraid I might still reject her after everything we'd shared over the last several days.

But I had no intention of breaking her heart. It was mine to protect, and I would protect it with everything I had.

"Completely," I murmured before sealing my lips over hers and kissing her, hoping she could feel the depth of that word in my kiss.

Rule #21

BOOKS CAN'T TURN YOU ON

Wyatt

For the last hour, we'd been dozing snuggled on the couch. It had started out innocently enough with her back to my front while she read one of her steamy books out loud. I had actually been pleasantly surprised that it wasn't all sex—there was a real story there. The characters were complex and there was even a scene where Brynn had started to tear up from the emotion the author was able to convey.

And then it got to a steamy scene, and I don't know if it was the beautiful woman in my arms or the words themselves, but I got hard thinking about recreating the scene with Brynn. Then my hands were on her body and she was giving me those breathy sighs she did when she was getting worked up. We were naked within minutes, me thrusting inside of her as she called out my name and once again came on my cock. She was beautiful in the throes of passion, and I was quickly getting addicted to the feel of her pussy convulsing around my cock when she came.

We'd collapsed entwined together on the couch and

neither of us had moved since. The sweat from our earlier exertion had dried by now, and I was relishing the simple feeling of her naked body pressed against mine. I didn't want to move, but I knew we'd need to make dinner soon and neither of us would want to do that with the feeling of dried sweat and the smell of sex on our bodies.

I slid my hand along her spine and watched as goose bumps followed the trail of my fingers. She stirred in my arms and kissed my chest.

"Come on. Let's get a shower and make some dinner."

I sat up and repositioned her so I could carry her like a bride to the bathroom. Once again, I could see our future so vividly—me carrying her exactly like this on our honeymoon, or even our wedding night in between bouts of sex. My blood heated thinking about the myriad of ways I could make this woman smile, laugh, and come in the future.

Even though the bathroom itself was relatively small, I was impressed with the size of the tub and shower. It was clear a lot of money had been put into this place to make it a home away from home. I set Brynn down only long enough to pull back the white shower curtain and get the water going, making sure it wasn't too hot. Once I found the perfect temp, I picked her back up—laughing when she squealed and smiled up at me—and stepped inside. Her lush pink lips were still tilted up in a smile as I set her on her feet and spun us so she was under the spray of the showerhead. I brushed my hands over her hair before lathering them with soap and massaging it gently into her hair. Her green eyes traced my face while I washed her hair, and her lips tilted up into an almost shy smile when I tipped her chin up with my finger so I could rinse it out.

I'd never done this for anyone else. The act felt more intimate than I'd anticipated, but it was satisfying on a bone-deep level. I knew no one took care of her like this, but she deserved to be cherished. It felt like the greatest honor I'd ever had to be the man who got to take care of her this way.

The man who finally got to help her relax and feel special.

I grabbed the washcloth draped over the side of the tub and squeezed some body wash on it before putting it under the water so I could get it lathered up. I took great care to wash every inch of her, starting from her neck and shoulders, down her arms to her fingertips, then over her chest and those beautiful breasts that always made my mouth water. I gently washed her stomach and then down between her legs, making sure not to linger there too long because I was worried she was a little sore from all of our activities.

While she hadn't complained about any of it, I was still well aware that we'd had more sex than either of us had in a long time. Despite my rigorous workout routines, my legs and back had gotten sore after a few of the more unique positions we'd tried. I couldn't imagine how she was feeling. I probably could've asked her and I trusted that she'd tell me, but part of taking care of her meant anticipating her needs without her having to always vocalize them. I'd studied her enough over the past couple of months that I'd worked with her that I knew most of her tells. But we hadn't been having sex then. I knew when she was hungry or tired, but I was still learning the signs that her body had hit its limits.

I got on my knees and washed down one leg all the way to her pink-painted toenails before I moved to the other leg and repeated the same process. I looked up at her to check in only to find her eyes shining with the hint of tears, but the emotions swimming in her eyes didn't make me think she was upset. She cupped my cheeks and bent down, kissing me soft and slow. They were drugging kisses that threatened to pull me under—if I hadn't already been held captive by her.

Unable to resist her, I stood up, wrapping her up in my arms and kissing her back, dragging the kiss out and getting lost in the taste of her. She broke the kiss first, and any threat of tears was now gone only to be replaced with hunger.

"My turn," she said with that sexy smile that had my dick harder than stone. She rotated us so I was the one under the water.

She pushed up on her toes in an attempt to shampoo my hair, and we both broke out into a little laugh when I had to duck down so she could reach. When she wore her heels, our height difference wasn't as noticeable, but in the shower, it was impossible to miss how petite she was at five foot seven compared to my six foot five. But I really couldn't complain about ducking down when it put me right at eye level of her perfect tits. The temptation was too much to pass up, and I sucked one of her pert nipples into my mouth, pinching it slightly with my teeth the way I knew she loved.

She let out a shuddering breath and then tugged my short hair. "Behave."

"Don't you know by now that's impossible when you're naked?"

Her smile spread across her face, and she just shook her head but stayed focused on her task. She really couldn't blame me. She was too tempting to pass up. Now that I'd had her so thoroughly, I didn't know how I'd ever found the strength to stay away for as long as I did. If I'd had any idea that it would be like this, I would've cracked the first night I caught her in the tub.

Although, maybe that wasn't entirely true because I didn't know her as well then as I did now. And it was knowing her—knowing all the little details about her and who she was as a person, not just how beautiful she was— that had pushed me over the edge. She was the most beautiful woman I'd ever met, inside and out.

When my hair was thoroughly lathered, she gave me permission to rinse it out while she got the washcloth ready with more body wash.

She started at my neck and shoulders just like I did for her, and with each brush of the cloth against my skin, I felt like she was taking more pieces of me—at least the pieces of my heart and soul I hadn't already given her over the last several days. No one had ever taken care of me like this either. I had never much thought about it, but now that I was experiencing it with her, my heart was beating double time, and gratitude filled me so strongly, it nearly brought me to my knees.

Her gaze followed the path of the washcloth as she washed down my abs, her tongue darting out across her bottom lip as she moved the material down to my hard cock.

She gave me a seductive smile and an arched brow. "You like what I'm doing to you." It wasn't a question.

"I love it," I choked out at the same time she gripped and tugged on my cock. It was the first time I'd used the L word, and while I wasn't saying—at least out loud—that I loved *her*, I still heard the way she inhaled sharply at my words. For a split second I wondered what she'd say if I told her I loved her. But then all thoughts were forgotten when she dropped to her knees and took my achingly hard cock in her wet mouth.

I slapped the wall next to me once and left my hand there, wishing there was something I could grip instead of the smooth white tile. "Fuck, baby."

She hummed as she licked me from base to tip and then swirled her devilish tongue around the head like she was licking around an ice cream cone. My fingers dove into her hair, not guiding her movements—she didn't need any help—but because I was desperate to touch her.

One of her hands gripped the base while she worked my tip in and out of her mouth, sucking as she pulled away.

"Fuck, that feels good."

I stared down at her with hooded eyes, my chest rising and falling rapidly the closer she brought me to the edge. "You take my cock so good, baby."

Like the fucking siren she was, she looked up at me with those beautiful green eyes and my cock in her mouth. There was heat and appreciation in her gaze and something else I was desperate to see, but couldn't vocalize in words yet.

She broke our eye contact, but I didn't protest because she followed it by taking my cock all the way to the back of her throat and swallowing. She gagged slightly from my size, but once she took a breath, she did it again. One of my hands stayed in her hair, but the other went to the side of her neck, my thumb resting on her throat where I could feel the movement of her swallowing against my finger.

"B-baby. I'm gonna come if you do that again."

In response, she gripped the back of my thighs and took me all the way deep in her throat. There was no way I could hold back any longer when she swallowed again, her throat constricting around my cock. With a shout, I came with an orgasm so intense it felt like my blood pressure spiked. When I finally caught my breath, I bent over, cupped her face in my hands, and kissed her hard, only breaking away because I was still catching my breath from the orgasm she'd literally sucked out of me.

"Fuck, you're a goddess."

A smile broke out on her face. I would do anything to make her smile like this for the rest of our lives. "That's what every woman deserves to hear after she gives her man a blow job."

I helped her up to standing and then held her tight against my body, angling us so the water could warm us both instead of just my back. I didn't want to let her go, and I could've happily stood there holding her until the water ran cold, but when her stomach rumbled, I knew I needed to make sure she got fed.

"Come on. Let's dry off and make some dinner."

Rule #22

DON'T FALL IN LOVE WITH YOUR BODYGUARD

Brynn

Wyatt's hand wrapped around my throat as he thrust into me from behind. His hips pistoned relentlessly as he held my body exactly where he wanted it. The pleasure was borderline too intense, but I knew that was the point. He was going to push my body to the very edge of what it could do—he'd already proved I could experience more pleasure than I knew was possible.

I wasn't inexperienced at sex, but most of my partners had preferred missionary. While Wyatt and I had done that position, there had been nothing tame or boring about it. He'd found other mild ways—like lightly pinching my clit or whispering filthy words in my ear—to make a typically vanilla position feel even more explosive.

I couldn't decide what position was my favorite when every single one managed to light my body up in ways I'd never experienced. In the time since we finally gave in to our desire for each other, Wyatt had traced every inch of my skin with his tongue, he'd run his callused fingers over every freckle, and he'd worshipped me to the point that I knew he'd ruined me for sex with anyone else.

Because there was no way anyone could ever make me feel even an eighth of what I'd grown to feel for Wyatt in such a short amount of time.

"Goddammit, your pussy feels so fucking good," he groaned against the back of my head as his fingers tightened —not enough to hurt or cut off my oxygen, but just enough to remind me that he had complete control of my body in this moment. The bliss this man made me feel was intoxicating.

At his words, I flexed my pelvic muscles and loved the way it made him shake behind me.

"Fuck," he cursed. "So damn good. Can't get enough."

I pinched my eyes closed as my core tightened in that way which had become so familiar during the time we'd been together at the cabin. "Oh God. I'm gonna c-come." The words were barely out of my mouth when my body began to shake and my pussy convulsed around his thick length.

He cursed again and then I felt the warmth of his release as he let go inside of me, his front pressed firmly against my back. We both had a sheen of sweat and would need another shower, but I didn't care. I'd never felt as good as I had the last several days with him. I sagged forward, only held up by his arm around my upper chest now that he'd moved his hand off my throat.

He placed a kiss against the back of my neck and then let me fall forward to the bed. My arms were still shaking from the pleasure overload, and I was just about to let myself fall completely into bed when he grabbed me and positioned us on our sides facing each other. He brushed my sweaty hair off my face and then his hand stilled against the side of my neck, his dark brown eyes staring at me with a slight furrow between his brows. He shook his head like he was shaking a thought away and then rolled to his back, draping an arm above his head and wrapping the other around me so he could hold me tight against him.

"What is it?" I asked, running a finger through his sparse brown chest hair. I'd only ever dated guys who shaved or waxed their chests, and I couldn't deny I loved how manly Wyatt's chest hair made him look.

"Nothing," he said, his voice deep, but his tone seemed troubled which belied his word.

I tilted my head to see him better. His brows were still furrowed, and his mouth was set in a thin line as he stared at the ceiling above us.

"Wyatt..."

He turned his head, his brows softening when he looked at my face, but there was now a hint of worry in his eyes as he stared at me. He moved the hand he'd draped above his head to cup my face. "I can't protect you like this."

"What do you mean?"

He shook his head and then looked back up at the ceiling. "If someone tried to get to you right now, I'd be essentially useless. You're all I can think about."

I smiled. "You say that like it's a bad thing."

My smile froze when he turned his serious expression on me. "It's a very dangerous thing. I should be on top of security and thinking about all possible outcomes. I should be alert and prepared for anything. But when I can only see you, only think about you, only crave your smile, your laugh, your body, it makes me a liability. I can't do the job I'm supposed to do. You're all I can see, and it's now a weakness, not a strength when it comes to your protection."

My smile fell completely by the time he'd finished talking. But my heart was racing a mile a minute in my chest. "What are you saying?"

His jaw clenched and a new worry swirled in my belly. He wouldn't end this right now, would he? He couldn't, not when he claimed to feel what he felt, right? I mean, he hadn't said the words, but I thought it had been obvious we were both falling hard for each other.

Now I wasn't so sure.

"I'm saying..." He looked back up at the ceiling. "I don't know what I'm saying. I can't stop. I don't want to," he reassured me, holding me tighter against him. And then he whispered, "My feelings for you make me a liability to you, when I'm supposed to be keeping you safe."

Neither of us said anything after that for a long time. Eventually, Wyatt dozed off, but I stayed awake, staring vacantly at the wall as I let his words run on repeat in my head. Most worrisome to me was that he was still thinking of me as a job at all when I'd long since stopped thinking of him as my bodyguard. My heart wanted him to be so much more than that. I was worried that it was too fast to have such strong feelings, but they hadn't started the minute we'd gotten physical—they'd been growing for weeks. Having sex just took them to a new high.

But now I was worried the strength of my feelings wasn't as reciprocated as I'd thought.

Rule #23

STAY INSIDE AT ALL TIMES

Wyatt

Our time at the cabin was already over halfway gone and yet I didn't think Brynn would make it any longer before going completely stir-crazy. We'd had more sex than I'd had in a year, and we'd played card games that inevitably turned into the "strip" version of whatever we were playing.

Strip poker, strip gin rummy, even strip Go Fish—once we'd gotten especially bored of poker and gin rummy.

We'd read books in front of the fire—well, she'd read to me from her tablet while I massaged her legs that rested in my lap. When it got to the steamy parts, we'd typically end up having sex on the couch or the floor.

It was impossible to keep our hands off each other for long. I didn't know if it was the confined space or the fact I'd just broken an abnormally long dry spell, or if it was just the power of our attraction to each other, but we both seemed to be affected equally. And I wasn't going to complain about off-the-wall-amazing sex.

I wrapped my arms around Brynn who was standing at

the kitchen sink staring out the small window. I'd avoided going outside unless I needed to chop wood because it was impossible to guarantee her safety outside of this cabin. Hell, with how fucked my head was over this woman, I couldn't say with one hundred percent certainty that I could guarantee her safety *in* the cabin either.

My job had quickly fallen to the wayside once we crossed that line—or blew it to smithereens, which seemed a more appropriate description. I cared more about her safety now than I ever had, and yet I felt more inadequate than ever to protect her the way she needed to be protected.

But right up there along with her safety, I cared about her overall well-being, and I could tell being stuck inside was weighing on her. We'd also had no contact with the outside world, something Raf insisted on because he hadn't discounted that the threat might very well be one of the few people she trusted the most. No one but Raf knew we were here, and no one but Raf had the ability to contact us.

Brynn needed an escape from our predicament and only I could give it to her. "Wanna go for a walk?" I murmured against her soft hair.

She spun around, her eyes wide. "Are you fucking with me right now?"

I laughed. "Nope. Thought maybe you'd want to get some fresh air, stretch your legs."

"I thought you said it wasn't safe."

I shifted my jaw. "It's not, or at least it's harder to guarantee it's safe. But Raf's got this place rigged with perimeter sensors and none of them have been tripped, so as long as we remain on the property, we should be okay. There's about two acres that are covered by the sensors. Both properties on either side of this one are also vacation homes and vacant right now. Raf got the owners' permission to put cameras on their properties for the time being so we could probably go a little farther into their lots if you want to walk more."

She grabbed my arm and stunned me stupid with a smile so bright it completely transformed her face to make her glow like an angel. "Let me go put on my shoes!"

She pushed up onto her toes and planted a quick kiss to my lips, then darted into the living room and up the stairs to the loft while I remained in the kitchen. I brushed my fingers over my lips and wondered if the awe that she always made me feel was normal.

Was this how Travis felt about Sadie? No wonder it had knocked him on his ass. I felt a bit knocked on my ass myself.

As much as I loved and craved sex with her, it wasn't just the sex that had my head a mess. I wanted to know everything about her, from the smallest details like how she took her morning coffee—two spoonfuls of French Vanilla coffee creamer or three spoonfuls of sugar and some milk in a pinch—to what her long-term dreams were. I wanted to make her laugh so hard she snorted. I wanted to be the shoulder she leaned on when she was having a bad day. I wanted to be the man she came home to at the end of every tour.

This wasn't lust. Lust was heady and fleeting. It didn't make my stomach bunch with thoughts of making a life with her and building a family if she wanted one. Lust didn't make me plan out my resignation letter in my head for the job I'd made my life since I got out of the navy.

I'd given up worrying if it was too soon to feel the big L word. I was gone for her. I'd fallen so hard in love with her, I knew there was no way I would ever be able to feel this way for someone else again.

But also saying it out loud was more terrifying than I'd expected it to be.

"Okay, I'm ready," she said, bouncing off the last step like a kid who'd just been given the go-ahead to jump in every puddle they could find after a hard rain. Her face had been free of the heavy makeup she wore for shows the whole time we'd been here, and I loved her fresh face and getting to see her this way. Her green eyes were bright with joy as she walked toward me, her expression open and eager.

"Let's go." I held my hand out for her, and she took it without hesitation which made me feel about ten feet tall.

My senses were on alert the second we exited the house, but it was hard to stay as focused as I knew I should've been when Brynn was practically bouncing on her toes with each step. She closed her eyes, tipped her head back, and breathed deep as we walked deeper into the woods.

"God, this is exactly what I needed," she said.

I smiled at the happiness in her voice. "I figured."

She faced me with a sly smile on her face. "Think you know me so well already, huh?"

"Oh, most definitely." I shrugged. "You're pretty predictable."

Her jaw dropped and she smacked me with the back of her hand. "Rude."

I grabbed her hand before she could move it and twirled her around, making her laugh. I pulled her tight against my body, wrapping my other arm around her waist and lowering my head until our noses almost touched. "See? I knew you'd laugh if I did that."

She rolled her eyes, and for once she truly looked her age. "I'd have to be heartless not to laugh when you twirled me by surprise." Her eyes sparked and the eyebrow over her right eye arched. She leaned forward until her lips brushed against the shell of my ear. "I bet you'd never expect me to do this…"

There was a moment's pause and then she nipped at my earlobe and took advantage of my surprise to dart away into the trees. My heart raced as worry and adrenaline battled for dominance the farther she got away from me, her laughter ringing through the trees.

And then something predatory spiked through my veins and I chased off after her. The trees were thicker here, but she wasn't as fast as I was. She could hide behind one, but she'd need to move at some point.

I also had another advantage on her—I'd been trained in tactical operations. I knew how to move in the space damn near silently.

If she wanted to play the prey, I'd hunt her down.

A branch cracked a few feet away, and I stealthily moved around a cluster of trees to come around on the right instead of the left where I suspected she'd be looking for me.

Her body was twisted as she glanced around the left side, her chest rising and falling with her rapid breaths from running. I came up behind her before she had a chance to twist around and wrapped my hand over her mouth to stifle her scream. Holding her close to my body, I dragged my nose delicately up her neck and then brushed my lips against her ear. "Think you can run from me?"

She huffed behind my hand, but the crinkles next to her eyes told me she was smiling.

"Don't you know I'll always find you?" I whispered.

She moved her body, and I let her go just enough that she could twist around. "Promise?" she asked, her voice low and throaty, her green gaze piercing my heart with the longing there.

"Always," I murmured. Then I crushed my lips to hers.

She moaned against my mouth, her body melting against mine. With every kiss, this woman owned more pieces of me. I didn't think there'd be anything left that didn't belong to her by the time we left Tahoe.

I gripped the back of her thighs and wrapped them around my hips as I moved forward, resting her back against the tree she'd been hiding behind. She rocked her hips against the hard length in my pants and moaned into my mouth. I'd never deny her anything she wanted, especially not when I wanted it too.

I put her down on her feet just enough so she could push her pants down and kick one foot out. While she was doing that, I undid the button on my jeans and pushed my pants and boxer briefs down to my knees. The second we were both ready, she wrapped her arms around my neck, and I lifted her up by her thighs. She didn't hesitate to wrap her legs back around my hips, crossing her ankles just above my ass.

Her pussy ground against my cock, the movement eased by her slick juices. "Fuck yeah, baby, rock your pussy against me just like that."

She whimpered, kissing me fiercely, her tongue darting into my mouth when I parted my lips. Fuck, it was a rush experiencing her like this. The urgency of her kiss combined with the frantic movement of her lower body and the way she tightened her arms and legs around me like she was afraid I'd stop her. I wouldn't. I'd never dream of it.

Someday—probably very soon—she'd realize that I had no plans to stop this ever.

"Wyatt," she moaned just as she rocked against me and

I slipped inside. Her pussy accommodated me instantly now, making way for my thick cock as I buried myself to the hilt. Her thighs shook around my hips and her breath stuttered. "Y-you feel so good inside me. So f-full."

Her eyes closed and her cheeks flushed pink. I was mesmerized, hypnotized, captivated in every possible way.

But I wanted her to come looking in my eyes. I wanted to see the pleasure streak across her face again and let her see it streak across mine when she ripped my orgasm from my body and took it into her own.

"Open your eyes for me, baby. Let me see all of you."

It seemed difficult for her, but then her eyelids lifted and we stared at each other as I thrust in and out, picking up the pace until we were both panting hard. I was close—too close—and needed her to come before me. Sliding a finger between us, I ran it over her plump clit, loving the way she sucked in a sharp breath and shuddered at the combined sensation.

"Wyatt," she screamed into the air as her pussy pulsed and tightened around me. I couldn't hold off any longer and let the pleasure shoot up my spine and through every nerve ending. My thrusts stuttered to a stop as I buried myself inside her as far as I could and let my cum fill her.

I'd never had sex without a condom before her, and after this trip, I wasn't sure I'd ever be able to wear one with her even once we had them available.

I was never going to let anything come between us.

Rule #24

ALWAYS EXPECT THE UNEXPECTED

Wyatt

A few days later, we were making spaghetti in the kitchen while an old Boyz II Men CD played on the stereo. Brynn had found it among a few other nineties era artists when she found the stereo and decided to play through those instead of trying to find a radio station that would come through clearly.

I was stirring the sauce on the stove while she cut up some broccoli to go with it. She swayed her hips and danced subtly, but it was enough to catch my eye. I couldn't have stopped the smile that bloomed on my face if I tried. This woman was more than I'd ever expected.

She caught me staring. "What?" she asked, her cheeks getting that subtle blush I'd grown so fond of over the past week and a half.

I shook my head but didn't stop staring. "Nothing. Just admiring the view."

Her lips tilted up in a smile, and she opened her mouth

to respond when a distinct ringing came from the living room. My smile fell as I dropped the stirring spoon onto the counter and rushed to the bag where the burner phone from Raf had been since we got here. I had plugged it into the wall to keep it fully charged and then tucked it into the side pocket, assuming I wouldn't need it for a couple more days to check in and make sure all was clear for us to come back.

He shouldn't be calling me now. It was too soon.

"Hello?" I answered.

"We caught him," he said without preamble.

I moved toward the window with the phone against my ear. The calm of the lake was a strange juxtaposition to the chaos inside me. "When?"

"Last night. He tried to break into her house. We had Jamie on site and he was able to incapacitate him until the police could arrive. He's in custody now. They're holding him on attempted breaking and entering and stalking. He had pictures of her along with a journal filled with some sick fantasies in the passenger seat of his car."

Something heavy swirled in my stomach—maybe doubt, maybe guilt because I knew Raf wouldn't be talking to me so calmly if he knew what I'd done. "And we're sure he's the same guy who left the notes?"

"You think she could have two stalkers at that level?"

"I'm just asking if there's any way to confirm. The notes weren't handwritten and had no DNA. Did he confess?"

He paused. "He hasn't yet, but my contacts with LAPD said he's been tight-lipped since they picked him up. He lawyered up immediately, and he has a pretty extensive record. This wouldn't be his first stalking offense." He took an audible breath. "I can't remember a time you've ever questioned me on something like this. What's different about this one?"

The heaviness in my stomach moved to my chest and my limbs, making my whole body feel weighted down. I was sure if someone pushed me into the lake right this second, I'd sink straight to the bottom.

Raf has been one of my closest friends for most of my adult life. After my brother, he was my best friend. I couldn't tell him the truth over the phone. He deserved a face-to-face confession. I needed him to see my eyes when I told him I'd crossed professional boundaries and fallen in love with a client.

"Wyatt? You still there?"

I cleared my throat. "Yeah, I'm still here. I didn't mean to question you. I know you take client safety seriously."

"I'd be horrible at my job if I didn't. Are you sure there's not something else going on?" He asked it like a mom who already knew the answer to the question, but was gauging to see if her kid would be honest.

"Nothing that can't wait until we get back. So if you caught him, does this mean we can come back sooner?"

"Yeah. In fact, her team is losing their damn minds and hoping you guys can come back tomorrow morning."

"Okay. We'll pack up tonight and leave first thing in the morning. It'll take us about eight hours or so to get back to LA depending on traffic."

"Perfect. I'll let her team know. Jamie will meet you at her place for a trade-off so you can get a well-deserved break. I hope she hasn't been too much of a diva for you."

I grinned at that. "Nah, she hasn't been a diva at all."

"Hmm," he replied in a way that made me wonder if I gave too much of my fondness for her away in my tone. "Well, I'll check in with you tomorrow or the day after."

"Sounds good. I appreciate you, man," I added, emotion clogging my throat. I hoped he'd forgive me. I'd seen how pissed he'd been when he fired the other guys who crossed the lines with clients. If his business got a bad reputation because his guys couldn't keep their dicks in their pants, no one would work with him. As it was, he worked with the elite of the elite and he didn't want to downgrade. His whole life revolved around his business, and I didn't know if he'd forgive me for further putting his reputation in jeopardy.

But I'd still choose Brynn over working for Raf, even if he never forgave me.

"I appreciate you too, Wyatt," he said, his words slowed like he wasn't sure what came over me. He'd find out soon enough because once we were back in LA, I didn't want to keep our relationship a secret. Jamie could take over for me as her bodyguard, but I'd be staying with her as her boyfriend until I was certain she was safe.

Despite Raf's claims, this didn't feel resolved. My gut was still tense, and I wasn't sure it was all about the lie I was keeping from him. But maybe I'd just become too pessimistic. Maybe Brynn would be able to break me of that.

I spun around and walked back into the kitchen where Brynn was stirring the sauce, her brows furrowed and her mouth a flat line.

"Uh-oh, you didn't burn the sauce, did you?" I teased. She'd shared that she was a notoriously bad cook.

But she didn't laugh or smile. There was none of the lightness we'd shared between us earlier.

Instead, she glanced up at me with resolve on her face, her features now composed like I'd seen when she was making decisions for her business.

"I've been thinking about when we go back."

"Okay. Well, the good news is it looks like we'll be heading back tomorrow. They caught the guy. You'll be safe now."

I moved forward and wrapped my arms around her. "Plus you'll always have me."

It registered a second late that she held her body stiff instead of melting into me like she normally did.

"Brynn?" I asked, pulling back.

She faced me, and in her beautiful eyes I could see the woman who made tough but crucial business decisions on a daily basis. It wasn't the ruthlessness I'd seen in the eyes of bigwig CEOs, but it had a similar sharpness that implied the decision had been made and nothing would change her mind.

"I think we should go back to you being my bodyguard and me being your client once we leave here."

Only because of a decade in the military and years in this business was I able to keep my facial expression neutral even as I felt her words like a bullet to the gut. And then she continued, each sentence another hit until I felt riddled with holes.

"This has been fun, and it was the exact distraction I needed. But I have too much to lose if people find out, and I need to focus on my music and the rest of the tour. I hope you understand."

She wasn't asking. She was telling. This wasn't a conversation between lovers about where things would go next. This was one person making an executive decision and breaking the other's heart. All this time I'd thought she was worried about *me* breaking *her* heart, when apparently I should've been worried about it being the other way around.

"If that's what you want," I said, keeping my voice impassive.

For the first time since I reentered the kitchen, doubt seemed to fill her eyes, but she blinked it away so quickly, I questioned if I really saw it.

Rule #25

DON'T MAKE DECISIONS FOR ANYONE BUT YOURSELF

Brynn

It took everything in me to keep the tears I felt from filling my eyes and falling. My chest felt like it had been ripped open, the jagged edges of my ribs filling the void where my heart had once been.

But I knew I'd made the right decision.

I'd only heard Wyatt's side of his conversation with Raf, but it was enough for it to really hit me and to realize what he was sacrificing if anyone found out we'd been together. I hadn't fully thought about the consequences when we were tucked away alone together, which wasn't like me at all. Usually I overthought those things. Ran through all the worst-case scenarios.

This time I'd followed my heart with blinders on, never thinking about what was coming at us from the side.

But reality—or that phone call rather—was a swift kick to the gut. If we stayed together, Wyatt wouldn't just be risking his job—which I knew he'd lose because the terms in the contract I signed were crystal clear that there should be zero fraternization—but he'd also lose a friend. The way he spoke to Raf and the way he'd spoken of him when he'd told me about his time in the military made it clear that friendship was important to him.

How could I allow him to risk all that when he had no idea about the reality of my life? If he was with me as a couple, he'd never have another moment of privacy. There'd always be cameras following him around. As my bodyguard, he could remain in the background. As my boyfriend, he'd never know peace again.

I couldn't do that to him, so instead I'd ended things, and he'd hardly spoken to me since. Not that it mattered. I couldn't talk over the lump in my throat that I was sure would turn into tears if I dared speak.

The drive back to LA was filled with a fraught and tense silence that had all my muscles bunched and aching by the time we neared my mansion. I should've felt relieved to finally have an escape, but my heart clenched painfully at the thought of Wyatt leaving.

Would he come back, or would he ask to be reassigned? What would I do if I never saw him again?

He parked the SUV. "Wait here."

He got out of the car, his eyes covered with his mirrored aviator sunglasses and his jaw set. His head twisted around in a way that told me he was assessing the surroundings. Then he was at my door, opening it with a coolness he'd never had with me before. I slid out of the car gracefully, aware that soon I'd be surrounded by all the people I paid and wouldn't get a chance to talk to him for who knew how long. My fingers twitched with the desire to reach out and touch him, but I stopped myself in case there were photographers hiding—wouldn't be the first time.

I tucked my chin to my chest and opened my purse so

anyone watching would think I was checking inside it for something. I kept my voice low and only for him. If I never saw him again, I needed him to know one thing. "I'm sorry, Wyatt." My voice was thick with emotion, those pesky tears I'd fought against so hard now burning my eyes. "These last twelve days have been the best of my life." And then even quieter, so quiet I wasn't sure he'd even hear them. "No one will ever compare to you."

If he heard those final words, he'd probably think I meant sexually. And while he was the best I'd ever had, it was how hard I'd fallen in love with him that I knew no one would ever come close to. No one would make me feel what this man did.

His jaw clenched, the muscle jumping, but otherwise he didn't move.

Giving him up was the hardest thing I'd ever done, and I wondered if I'd always have to live with the hollowness I now felt knowing he couldn't be mine anymore.

My front door opened and my people flowed out, shouting at me, rushing over to me.

They all talked over each other, and while I could normally figure out what they were saying and address each in turn, I found myself feeling exhausted and tuning them out. I wanted so desperately to look over at Wyatt, to take off my own sunglasses and let him see the pain in my eyes so he'd know this was killing me. But I couldn't, because that was a luxury for other people.

I had all the money I could ever want, and it couldn't buy me the one thing I craved—the ability to enjoy my life in private, to even have a relatively normal life. To love the man I wanted without making his life worse.

Stella pulled me toward the front door, her assistant next to her. My tour manager was also here, along with the tour costume designer and several other people. Stella started talking the loudest, telling me how grateful she was that this madness was all over and we could get back to work. I almost laughed because this "madness" as she called it would never be over. Maybe this stalker was taken care of, but there would likely be another in the future.

This madness was my life and I'd never be free of it.

She went on and on about how they needed my sign-off on a few things before we started the next leg of the tour.

They pulled me into the house, and I glanced back before we made it to the living room. Wyatt stood at the threshold of the front door, talking to Jamie. His sunglasses were off now, but his eyes never glanced my way.

I silently begged for just one more look. I just needed him to look at me one more time like I mattered to him.

Jamie patted him on his upper arm, and Wyatt turned around without a single look my way. I stared, broken, lonely, and raw as Jamie closed the door.

I'd done the right thing saving Wyatt from this life. And yet everything about it felt wrong.

Rule #26

DON'T SHOW YOUR EMOTIONS

Wyatt

I should've driven straight home. I wasn't in a good headspace to be around people, but instead of going home, I drove to my brother's house. Two quick knocks and then I waited, staring vacantly at Travis's cement front porch and the welcome mat that screamed Sadie. My brother had never cared about things like a welcome mat, so it had to be his wife.

The door opened, light spilling out into the dusk as the sun started to set, and I looked up into my brother's concerned eyes. His gaze darted around my face and he immediately stepped out. "What's wrong?"

I shook my head. My throat was clogged with an emotion I wasn't sure I'd ever felt before. I'd experienced loss before, but it had never felt like this. I felt like I left a piece of myself on Brynn's driveway and the rest of me back at the cabin where I'd experienced the highest high of my life and then the lowest low.

Travis gripped my bicep and then moved his hand

around to my back and ushered me into his house. Sadie was curled up on the couch, a tablet in her lap. She straightened and her brows furrowed the closer I got to her. "Are you okay?"

I sat on the couch on the opposite end from her. My body felt too heavy to hold up any longer, and I bent over, resting my elbows on my knees and my head in my hands. "No," I admitted.

I was far from okay. Yesterday I thought I'd been in love and was willing to throw away my whole career. Today, I felt empty and broken, and I was pretty sure my job was going to be the only reason to get up in the morning. I knew Raf still deserved the truth, but I couldn't tell him. Not now. Not when it didn't matter anyway. She'd ended things swiftly and seemed confident in her decision.

Hell, she hadn't said a word to me on the drive back. Just that apology when she stepped out and something else she'd mumbled too low for me to hear. I hadn't asked her what she said because I didn't think I could take anymore.

"Got a beer?" I asked my brother. I rarely drank, but tonight seemed like a good time to drink away my problems. I was too old to get away with drinking much without feeling the effects in the morning, but the pain of a hangover might be more tolerable than the pain I felt in my chest.

"Only if you're planning to crash in the guest room," he replied.

I gave one nod and he turned to head to the kitchen.

"A girl?" Sadie asked, her sweet voice soft.

"A woman," I corrected. My niece, Jenna, had scolded me once when I referred to a woman I was casually seeing as a girl and went off on a whole tangent about how they're women and should be respected by being referred to as such. You'd never refer to a grown man as a "boy" unless you were being condescending. Her lecture had stuck with me and I found myself correcting everyone around me whenever the term was used that way.

"Ah, Jenna gave you the lecture," Sadie said, and when I glanced over, she had a fond smile on her face. She was Jenna's best friend, and it had been a big deal when she started hooking up with Trav behind Jenna's back. It had messed with both of their heads, but everything had worked out in the end.

I'd never really been jealous of my brother, but I was right then. He'd gotten his well-deserved happily ever after while I was contemplating which was worse—remaining on Brynn's detail and pretending nothing happened between us while acid ate away at my heart every second I couldn't touch her, or walking away and asking for a reassignment which meant never seeing her again.

Both options were painful.

Thankfully, Raf had given me a few days off which meant I had time to wrap my head around everything and decide what to do.

Travis came back into the room with two beers and a bottle of water. He handed a beer to me and the water to Sadie. I arched a brow at her, and the subtle blush and way she ducked her head gave her away.

"How far along are you?"

She shook her head and looked at her husband with exasperation. "You knew he'd figure it out if I didn't drink."

Travis shrugged unapologetically. "You haven't had enough water today." He leaned over her, trapping her body between his arms. "I gotta take care of my baby while she takes care of our baby."

I looked away when he kissed her. My heart clenched painfully tight. I wanted that, more than I'd ever allowed myself to admit before. I wanted a wife and kids—a family of my own. But not with just anyone. I wanted it with Brynn.

Did Brynn even want kids?

It was a stupid thought to have since she'd ended things, and it didn't matter that I'd never asked her. For a second I wondered if having the answer would make me get over her faster, but I knew in my gut it wouldn't matter if she didn't want kids. I'd still want her. She'd be my family and that would be enough.

"You gonna tell me what's going on?" Trav's voice pulled me out of my depressing thoughts.

I glanced up to find him sitting in the chair across from me and Sadie sipping at her water. They both looked at me, patiently waiting for me to tell them why I'd randomly shown up on their doorstep on a weeknight.

"I fell in love with a client who's thirteen years younger than I am and completely out of my league. Yesterday she ended things like it all meant nothing to her." The words poured out of me. I was used to being vulnerable with my brother, but doing it in front of Sadie was new. I wasn't opposed to a woman's perspective though, especially considering she once had been the younger woman in a seemingly forbidden pairing.

Travis sat forward, setting his beer on the table next to him before focusing on me. "I'm sorry. I'm going to need you to back up. Did you just say you fell in love with her? The last time we'd talked, you'd only said you found her attractive."

I blew out a puff of air and ran my hands through my hair. "Yeah, well, it became a lot more than that."

"Fuck," he muttered.

"Pretty much," I said.

"Does Raf know?" he asked.

I shook my head, and that sick feeling swirled in my stomach again.

"Why'd she end it?" Sadie asked.

"She didn't think it was worth the risk, I guess." The words came out rough.

It was hard to think about that moment when she ripped the rug out from under me. I'd spent nearly two weeks thinking we were well on our way to something serious. We'd both clearly fought the attraction that had been brewing ever since we met. But during our time in Tahoe, it felt like so much more than that. There was a depth to our conversations that I'd never had with anyone else. Quiet moments in the dark when we were curled up in bed together sharing secrets we'd never shared with anyone else —at least that had been the case for me.

Had I misread the situation that badly? Maybe that's why I felt so thrown—I'd never been so wrong about someone before. I'd never taken such a needless risk and had not expected for it to blow up in my face so spectacularly.

Travis rubbed his chin. "I'm still wrapping my mind around the fact you took that risk in the first place. Was she really worth risking your job and potentially your friendship with Raf? He'll be pissed if he finds out."

I looked at him pointedly. "I don't know. Was it worth risking your relationship with your daughter when you started hooking up with her best friend?"

His jaw dropped, and I only felt slightly guilty. He didn't look away from me when he spoke next. "Sadie, can you give me a minute with Wyatt?"

She got up and gave him a quick kiss and then turned to me. "It was worth it. I don't know this girl or any of the details obviously, but I know you pretty well. If you thought she was worth the risk, ask yourself why she might've pulled back. Did you say or do something that made her question the situation? And try to look at it from her point of view and consider if there was something that made her realize what *you* would lose by being with her. Just food for thought."

She exited the living room, heading upstairs to their bedroom. Travis and I stared silently at each other until we heard their door close, but even in the silence I could tell my brother was pissed at me. His eyes had gone hard and his jaw was clenched.

His voice was low. "Don't ever fucking question if the risk was worth it for the life I have with Sadie."

I ducked my head. "I'm sorry. You're right; that was uncalled for."

"Does this woman mean that much to you?"

I respected my brother enough to look him in the eye when I answered. "Yes." I scrubbed my hands over my face. "I've never fallen for anyone this hard or this quickly."

"So what are you gonna do? Can you still work with her? Do you even want to?"

"I don't know. I don't know anything," I said, my body sagging back against the couch cushions.

And I had no idea if a few days would be enough for me to forget what it felt like to touch her, to hold her, to feel whole.

I wasn't sure a lifetime would be enough time.

Rule #27

DON'T INTERRUPT HER SHOW

Wyatt

I decided she was worth the pain. It was worth staying on her service to know she was safe. No one would care about her protection the way I would, and if all I got from here on out was to watch her shine from behind the scenes, it would have to be enough.

The alternative was never seeing her again, and that hurt worse than not being able to touch her but still being close.

Maybe I'd been a masochist in another life.

Jamie greeted me with a smile when he opened her front door. "Enjoy your days off?"

I stepped inside, my gaze already scanning the room for Brynn. "Yeah, it was alright."

It was the worst three days of my life, and I couldn't wait to lay my eyes on Brynn again. There'd been a knot in my stomach since I left her, and only the sight of her safe would ease it.

We walked down the hall and into her huge kitchen

where Stella was yammering on while she pointed to things on a tablet. Brynn was drinking out of a coffee mug, her gaze staring vacantly out onto the patio while she nodded along. I suspected she wasn't actually listening to her manager. She seemed too lost in her thoughts.

Jamie cleared his throat. "Wyatt and I are trading off." Her gaze shot from the patio to mine in a heartbeat, and I could've sworn relief filled her gorgeous green gaze that I'd pictured every time I closed my eyes.

Jamie clapped me on the back and then turned around and exited the same way I'd entered.

Brynn and I stared at each other, neither of us saying a word, but the energy between us grew and expanded, sparking like electricity.

Stella interrupted our moment, her gaze fortunately focused on her tablet and her watch. "Damn, where does the time go? Brynn, we need to get you to the venue for tonight's show."

Brynn blinked and her face morphed into that professionally neutral expression she seemed to wear the most. It was void of the passion she'd had on her face when we'd been together. The way her smile was so bright it seemed to light up the whole room and her eyes would practically glitter. There was none of that now. If she wasn't so beautiful, she'd look like any other corporate CEO walking into a boardroom.

Only her boardroom was a stage, and it hit me all at once that she was a performer. Not in the sense of her actual job title, but in the way she always seemed to be performing some role with her staff or her dancers or anyone she interacted with. The first time I'd seen her with her guard down was at the cabin.

She hadn't been performing then.

Sadie's words from three nights ago came back to me. She'd asked if Brynn had a reason for ending things. Was it this? Her life? The fact she always had to be "on" for someone? Did she think I wouldn't want to be with her in this chaos?

Did she think I couldn't handle her fame? Or that it would become too much for me?

How often had the past men in her life proved to be inadequate when it came to her lifestyle, including the parts she couldn't control?

I looked at her through a new lens. She seemed exhausted with bags under her eyes and the corners of her mouth turned down more than usual. Had she slept as poorly as I had the last few days?

I sat in the passenger seat as we made our way to the venue, the driver another one of Raf's guys who I'd worked with occasionally. It took more restraint than I knew I had not to constantly look back and check on her. As it was, my ears were attuned to her every sound. The soft cadence of her voice as she spoke to Stella. The way her body shifted on the expensive leather upholstery. The slight catch in her breath when she said my name.

Turning around, I met her vivid green eyes. "Yes?"

She swallowed once, her throat moving with the motion. "Is everything good with security at the venue?"

"Yes, ma'am."

I didn't imagine the slight wince at my returning to the formality I'd used before our time in Tahoe.

"Same rules as before. Anyone coming to the meet and greet has already been vetted. We also did background checks on all ticket holders who got floor seats."

Stella frowned. "Is that really necessary since she's not being threatened anymore?"

"Yes," I said, my voice cold and tone hard.

If I'd had my way, it would've been extended to anyone who bought tickets period, but Raf was concerned with a close attack. It would be nearly impossible to get a long-range weapon into tonight's venue. It was the "nearly" that made me grind my teeth. Raf had wanted to pull back the added security measures since we already had her stalker in custody. I'd been the one to put my foot down and demand it all stay in place.

I faced forward and they resumed their conversation for the remainder of the drive.

I was always amazed at the moving parts that went into a professional show of this caliber. But Brynn's shows seemed to have more moving parts than normal. The costumes and props, the band equipment, the literal mechanics she had going on as well. It was impressive but also utter chaos, and chaos always made me uneasy.

It was easy to miss little things in this level of madness. And often it was the smallest thing that could alert you to danger.

I was scanning the audience from my spot backstage. It wasn't ideal because there were blind spots, but it allowed me a decent view and kept me close to her if I needed to get to her quickly. Another bodyguard was stationed on the other side of the stage to cover the blind spots I couldn't see from my position.

She started singing one of her slow songs, and I'd seen her perform enough times now to know exactly when there were supposed to be flashing lights.

The one that caught my attention wasn't part of the

show. I narrowed my view while I hit my earpiece to communicate with the other bodyguard.

All my senses hyperfocused, and before I'd consciously made a decision, I was already rushing onto the stage. The crowd saw me before Brynn did, but the fingers all pointing behind her caused her to turn around.

Her eyes widened when she saw me rushing toward her, but she didn't hesitate or question my movements. She ran straight toward me, and I loved her so much more in that single second than I'd ever loved anyone. Her complete trust in me when I knew how important these shows were to her was something I'd never fully appreciated before.

She jumped into my arms and I spun my body, shielding her from the audience just as a burn of pain flared in my back.

Get her to safety.

It was the only thought in my brain as I ran off the stage, my steps faltering the closer I got to the backstage area where she'd be completely shielded from view of the audience. I could already hear the other bodyguard in my ear saying he'd called in reinforcements.

My pulse raced as my vision started to waver. The effects of the blood loss were swift, which wasn't a good thing. I squeezed my arms around her tighter. Would this be the last time I ever held her in my arms?

We made it to the darkened backstage, the stage manager standing by with her cellphone to her ear and talking quickly to someone on the other end. I set Brynn down and then staggered a step before collapsing to the floor.

Black tinged my vision, but I could still see well enough to watch Brynn fall to her knees, her terrified eyes staring at her bloody hand. Her gaze shot to me as everyone rushed around us. She leaned over me, grabbing my face until all I could see was her.

Tears filled her beautiful eyes and spilled down her pale cheeks. She was shaking her head. "No. No, no, no. You can't leave me, not like this. Please," her voice broke.

I ached to touch her face, to feel her smooth skin underneath my rough palms one last time, but no matter how hard I tried, I couldn't find the energy to lift my arm.

"You were worth it," I said, the words coming out a hoarse whisper that I hoped she heard.

And then everything faded to black.

Rule #28

NEVER SHOW WEAKNESS

Brynn

There were one hundred and twenty-seven ceiling tiles in this hospital room. I hated that I'd had enough time to count them all, but if I kept staring at Wyatt, silently begging him to wake up, I was sure his brother would pick up that I was more than just a grateful client whose life Wyatt had saved. As it was, I hadn't stopped holding Wyatt's hand unless I had to use the restroom or the nurse needed to check him. I was especially grateful that Travis hadn't asked me to leave when they'd given updates about his injuries since I wasn't family.

They'd been able to remove the bullet, but he'd lost a lot of blood and there'd been some minor damage they needed to repair. But overall, he'd gotten very lucky that it missed anything major.

With every second that passed with his eyes still closed, one thought kept permeating my mind on a painful endless loop. *I could've lost him.*

If Wyatt had died, he never would've known that I loved him, that being apart was killing me, that my resolve to keep him at a distance for his own sake was melting faster than an ice cube on cement on a hot summer day.

He needed to wake up. He needed to know I hadn't meant a single word I'd said before we left Tahoe. He needed to know he wasn't just my bodyguard.

He was so much more—he held my heart and my happiness in his hands.

My fingers twitched with the desire to brush the short strand of hair off his forehead. He had dark purple bags under his eyes, and his cheeks looked more sallow than they should. His mouth was slack, but he was breathing on his own. The doctor had assured Travis that Wyatt would pull through. It was just a waiting game at this point.

I'd never been a very patient person, but I found it even harder to be patient now. There were things that needed to be said. I needed to fix things between us.

"*You're* the client." It was the first time Travis had spoken to me since the doctor left.

I shifted my body to face him without letting go of Wyatt's hand. "The client he saved, yeah." I thought he already knew that. Why else would I be here by his bedside refusing to leave?

The corner of his lips tilted up slightly at the corner. "But not *just* the client he saved. You're the woman he wanted to quit for."

All the breath seized in my lungs. He told his brother? I knew how much his brother meant to him. He'd talked in depth about Travis and shared stories about them growing up. He'd said Travis was his best friend. My heart clenched painfully as it hit me how stupid I'd been. I should've talked to him about what he was signing up for before making an executive decision to end things. I should've done so much differently.

He sat forward, resting his elbows on his knees. "He came to my house after you guys got back from Tahoe." His gaze shifted to Wyatt, the slight smile on his face falling before he refocused on me. "I've never seen my brother that wrecked over a woman."

Pain hit me hard and intense like I'd just been hit by a semitruck on the freeway. I dropped my gaze to the ground as guilt ate away at me. Even after I ended things, he was considering quitting?

I glanced up at Wyatt, my heart aching in my chest.

"Are you in love with my brother?" I spun back around to find Travis scrutinizing me. "Because if you're not, then I don't think you should be here when he wakes up. Don't give him hope when there isn't any."

Hope? Did that mean he thought Wyatt would want me back?

I opened my mouth, but closed it and reconsidered what I wanted to say. "I'm not leaving."

I refused to say those three words to him and confess my true feelings before I confessed them to Wyatt. Those words were for him alone.

Travis seemed to understand. He nodded and then sat back, pulling his phone out of his pocket. "Mind if I step out for a minute? I gotta call my wife."

"Sure." I had no intention of leaving this room unless it was with Wyatt once he was discharged. Travis had instilled new hope in me, and I held on to it tightly.

Now that we were alone, I gave in to the urge and leaned forward, reaching out to brush aside the hair on his forehead. I pressed a gentle kiss to his lips, then rested my forehead on his with my eyes closed. "Please wake up."

He hummed and I sat back, holding my breath. His eyes opened slowly, and he blinked a few times before he spoke. "Am I dreaming?" His voice was rough and scratchy, but he was awake and he was alive and there was no way I could've stopped the tears if I'd tried.

He lifted his hand, cupping my cheek, his thumb brushing away an errant tear. "Don't cry, baby."

Another sob escaped at the pet name, and all the words I'd held in came tumbling out. "I'm so sorry, Wyatt. I didn't mean any of the things I said in Tahoe. I miss you so much. I don't want to be apart and I know that risks your job and being with me is most people's literal nightmare because the press are vultures and you'll never know a moment's peace again and—"

He pressed a finger to my lips as his mouth split into a wide grin. "You're worth it, Brynn. You're worth all the crazy I'll have to put up with. You're worth everything."

"I love you," I whispered. It was probably too soon to say those words, but that didn't make them any less true. His smile only broadened.

"Good, because I love you too."

I was closing the distance between us to kiss him again when the door opened and Rafferty Carmichael walked through. I recognized him instantly from the Carmichael Security website Stella had showed me when she hired them as my protection. He was imposing with his height and that stern, hawk-like gaze. Not many people intimidated me, but Rafferty Carmichael did. His gaze dropped to where my fingers were intertwined with Wyatt's, and his dark brow arched. His gaze focused on Wyatt, and something passed silently between them. Wyatt's smile was nowhere to be found now.

He squeezed my hand once before breaking the stare off with Rafferty to look at me. "Can you give me and Raf a minute alone?"

I nodded and then quietly walked out, hoping I hadn't just screwed things up for Wyatt already.

Rule #29

YOUR BOSS CAN'T ALSO BE YOUR FRIEND

Wyatt

The door had barely shut behind Brynn when Raf spoke. "Were you planning on telling me that you'd broken my number one rule?"

"In fact, I was."

"When? Before your service with her ended, or after? Because I'm assuming this didn't all happen after you were shot."

His tone was even, but I knew him well enough to know he was pissed. His tone was always curt and to the point whenever he was well and truly pissed off. I wasn't sure if it was from his upper-class breeding or because he'd been told to never show emotions, but it was a trait he always wielded to his advantage.

"It happened in Tahoe." I wasn't going to lie to him. "That's when we crossed the line, although feelings had been growing on both sides from the start." At least for me. I wasn't entirely sure when Brynn's feelings started. I knew she'd been sexually attracted to me early on—catching her with my name on her lips while she masturbated had given that one away. But it was clear in Tahoe that what we had was more than just attraction.

There was a bone-deep chemistry between us that had been impossible to deny.

"I'll resign," I said.

"You sure you want to give this up for her? She could drop you tomorrow and then what would you have?"

His response surprised me. "You mean, you aren't firing me?"

He moved over to the chair Brynn had occupied and dropped down, his body seemingly weighted down with the burdens he carried. He rubbed a hand over his face. "I should. I absolutely should fire you immediately for breach of contract at the bare minimum, but no, Wyatt. I wouldn't fire you. If you want to leave on your own accord, I can't stop you. But I do want you to ask yourself if she's worth it. You know what comes with being with her?"

Yeah, I knew. I'd been living it in the background, watching the chaos she had to deal with on a daily basis. It had only shown me how strong she really was to put up with that day in and day out. I knew our relationship would bring an even more insane deluge of media coverage.

I also knew she was worth it, and that she deserved to have someone who wanted her for her. Someone who didn't care about her money, her fame, or anything else. Just her.

Raf frowned, but before he could scold me anymore I had one critical question.

"Who was it?"

"That shot you?" At my nod, he continued. "Her name is Eliza."

My eyes widened. "It was a woman?" While not

unheard of, it was certainly rare, especially in this case. Women stalkers usually stalked men, not other women.

"She's a crazed fan of Brynn's ex. She didn't like that Brynn hurt him." He rolled his eyes. We both knew how the media had let that one play out. Despite both parties saying it was an amicable split, he'd let rumors circulate that Brynn had broken his heart.

"You got her? For real this time."

He winced but nodded. "The fans around her tackled her to the ground once they realized what she'd tried to do. They didn't take kindly to her trying to kill their favorite singer."

Brynn was so much more than that, but I wasn't going to argue about semantics. I was just grateful the whole ordeal was done. I didn't doubt there might be others in the future, but at least this one we could put firmly behind us.

"She confessed to everything like she was some martyr standing up for a cause. Her brother-in-law is a celebrity photographer who'd been following Brynn closely. That's how she knew about the studio and the hotel Brynn was staying at. But charges are being filed for attempted murder since she actually took a shot at Brynn. With her confession, there's no doubt she'll serve time. Even though there's no longer a direct threat, Stella has requested Carmichael Security stay on as Brynn's protection for the foreseeable future."

Raf stood up and brushed his hand down his already straight tie. His tailored suit was immaculate as always, but the frown on his usually neutral face was rare. "If you're serious about this, I'll need your formal resignation in writing for HR."

"I'll get it to you." He'd said he wasn't going to fire me,

but he knew I wouldn't stay anyway. My place was beside Brynn now, not as her bodyguard, but as her partner.

"And you're sure?" There was a note of something in his voice, like this was the end of a chapter he wasn't ready to close. And I suppose it was. We'd worked together most of our adult lives. He'd saved my ass probably as many times as I'd saved his.

I kept my tone soft, but my voice loud and clear. "I've never been more sure."

He nodded once and clapped me gently on the shoulder. Then he walked to the door, but stopped with his hand on the handle. He turned his face back to me, a sly grin on his face. "Invite me to the wedding, yeah?"

I smiled wide. "Will do, brother."

He opened the door and stepped back to make room for Brynn. "He's all yours," he said to her before he walked out without another backward glance.

Brynn stared at the now closed door before she looked back at me. "Is everything okay?"

I patted the mattress next to my leg as she came over and sat down, but that wasn't close enough for my liking, so I pulled her down until she was snuggled next to me. The bed was a tad too small for both of us, especially with my big frame, but we made it work.

"He knows," I said in answer to her question. She tilted her head back to look at me better, her beautiful green eyes wide and filled with worry. But before she could say anything, I kept going. "I told him I'm resigning from Carmichael."

"What? No, Wyatt, you can't do that. You love that job—"

"I love you more," I cut her off.

Her eyes filled with tears. "I love you too, but I don't

want you to someday resent me because you had to quit the job you loved."

"I won't."

"How do you know?"

The answer was easy, but one I'd never admitted out loud. "Because I never loved that job. It fell in my lap when I needed something, and I was good at it, so I kept doing it. But it was just a job, and I'll get another one. Maybe I can do something with my wood carvings like you suggested."

She smiled and then snuggled against me. Her delicate fingers traced over my chest. "So if you're not my bodyguard anymore, then what are you?"

I smiled, and despite the pain from my gunshot wound, I felt whole in a way I never had. "I'm yours."

Rule #30

YOU CAN'T BUY HAPPINESS

Brynn

ONE YEAR LATER

The cabin was exactly as I remembered it. The steep A-frame, the wall of windows, the glorious view of the pristine turquoise lake. I took a deep breath of fresh mountain air and felt the weight of expectation slip from my shoulders.

"Feel good to be back?" Wyatt asked as he set our bags down by the door.

"It feels amazing," I said, leaning back into his chest as his arms wrapped around me from behind, both of us staring out at the water.

When he'd brought up the idea of a well-earned vacation after the conclusion of my tour, I'd suggested somewhere tropical where I could rent out the whole resort and we could invite all our family and friends. But then he'd mentioned coming back here, just the two of us, and it was too tempting to resist.

This cabin had changed my life in a way I would never take for granted. And Wyatt had been right that we needed a vacation—just the two of us—where I could really let my guard down and relax. Having someone look out for my well-being who wasn't paid to be there was a new and unique experience I was still getting used to. Stella rarely reminded me to drink water, eat a snack before I faded, or thought about my vacation plans.

Wyatt took care of me in all the ways a true partner should. He was always watching, always making sure my needs were met.

"This vacation was such a good idea," I whispered, almost afraid to break the serenity in the silence.

"You deserved it after all the work you put in this last year. Have I told you lately how incredible you are?"

I smiled, my heart feeling fuller than I'd ever remembered. "Not today." But he told me often enough.

It was hard to remember what my life was like before him. Being with Wyatt was unlike any other relationship in my past. He was my lover, my best friend, my confidant. He lifted my spirits when they were low, held my hand when I needed strength, gave me his shoulder when I needed a good cry, and cheered the loudest whenever I succeeded. That wasn't to say that everything was perfect because that would be unrealistic. He still occasionally forgot to put the toilet seat down, and he more often than not left a towel on the floor after his shower. But his imperfections fit with my imperfections. More than that, I knew I could wholeheartedly be myself with him, whether that was with perfect makeup and fancy clothes, or my hair a greasy mess in a knot on the top of my head and wearing a ratty old T-shirt.

We complemented each other in all the ways that made us our best selves when we were together. If the last year had taught me anything, it was that we could weather any storm as long as we always fought together.

He'd given me a happily ever after that I'd long thought was out of reach for someone of my fame.

And it had all started right here in this very cabin.

Wyatt dropped a kiss to my head. "I don't think I can wait any longer," he murmured against my ear as he stepped back.

My head tilted back in a boisterous laugh as I spun around to face him and tease him about his libido. My laugh died in the air as I sucked in a sharp breath when I found him down on one knee, with a small heart-shaped wooden box in his hand.

He stared at me with love shining in those dark brown eyes of his. I would never get tired of having him look at me like that. "I love you so much. Brynn, you've changed my life in ways I never could've imagined, and I never want to go back to life before you. I want to be your partner in every way. I want to spend the rest of my life cheering you on and watching you conquer the world. Will you marry me?"

"Yes!" I whispered, my voice too choked up to be any louder. Then I leaned down and cupped his face in my hands and kissed him hard.

He pulled back just enough to slide the gorgeous ring on my finger before his lips were on mine again, kissing me fiercely, owning my mouth in the way only he could. He stood up and in one smooth movement lifted me up. My legs wrapped around his hips as he carried me inside, our kiss growing ravenous. It was like this cabin was our own personal aphrodisiac. He dropped me back over the arm of the couch and pulled down my pants, kissing every exposed inch of skin until he'd stripped me of my shoes, leggings, and underwear. He pushed my knees wide and stared down at my glistening sex.

"Fuck, I love how wet you get for me." His heated eyes connected with mine. "This pussy is mine."

"Yours," I confirmed. It would always only be his. Every part of me belonged to this man.

His smile grew wicked as he reached behind his neck and pulled his shirt off. He knew that move always turned me into a puddle of goo. It had to be the sexiest move a man could make, especially when it revealed a body as ripped as Wyatt's. My breath grew labored when he dropped to his knees and started to trail kisses from my thigh toward my aching clit. When he was just a breath away from where I wanted him, he moved to my other thigh, giving it the same treatment.

When he finally reached my dripping center, he let out a deep groan. "I could die between these thighs and I'd be a very happy man."

I gripped his hair hard until his gaze shot to mine. "Not for a very long time, understand?"

He smiled. "As my wife wishes."

My heart clenched at hearing him call me his wife. I was certain I'd never tire of that title.

Then, without breaking our gaze, he dropped his mouth down to lick up the seam of my pussy, and all thoughts disappeared. All that was left was the need to come. His tongue swirled teasingly around my clit before he wrapped those perfect lips of his around it and sucked. He kept up the sucking motion as he thrust two fingers inside me, and I detonated with a scream, my orgasm ripping through me.

I'd barely come down from the high when he shoved his pants down and thrust his thick cock inside me, causing both of us to groan at the connection.

"Fuck, Wyatt."

"That's it, Wife. Say my name while I make you come all over this cock again."

I let out a groan, wrapped a hand around his neck, and pulled his mouth to mine. His pace picked up, both of us eager to find our release together. We were both sweaty and breathing heavy when he slid a hand between us to rub circles over my clit. It was the exact amount of pressure I needed to send me over the edge again, and I came screaming his name as my pussy convulsed around him. He thrust twice more, his movements jerky before he stilled and came, buried deep inside me.

He sagged on top of me as he kissed me, this time sweetly. "I'll never get enough of you."

"Good," I said, kissing him again, loving how he still tasted a little like me.

"I love this cabin," I said on an exhale.

"Good, because I bought it."

I pushed him back so I could see his face and determine if he was serious. His smile was wide and his eyes had lost the stress they usually carried. This cabin relaxed him as much as it relaxed me.

"Did you really?" My tone gave away how hopeful I was that he was serious.

He nodded. "We need a place that's just ours to escape to when life gets too chaotic. I couldn't think of a better place than where I fell in love with you."

He pulled me up and then carried me up to the loft where we spent the rest of the day making love in our new cabin.

And I'd never been happier.

Bonus Rule

YOU CAN'T HAVE SEX ON FAMILY VACATION

Wyatt

TEN YEARS LATER

Squeals of laughter greeted my ears as I stepped out onto the deck. Brynn was teaching our youngest son, Adam, how to swim while his older brother, Dylan, watched from the dock I'd built. We spent at least two weeks here in Tahoe every summer as a family and it was easily our favorite two weeks of the year. We'd had to add on to the cabin to make room for all four of us, but it had been worth it to share the magic of the mountains and the lake with our ever-curious boys. Brynn and I also both agreed it was good for us all to disconnect and get away from the city every once in a while.

Brynn had wanted a big family—something I'd been fully on board with—but after she experienced complications with our second child, we decided having more wasn't worth the risk. Our family of four felt complete.

I leaned my forearms on the deck railing, watching my family. My boys were the spitting image of me, and I already loved how close they were. They reminded me a lot of Travis and myself when we'd been kids. The only difference was that my boys had two parents who would drop everything for them. Brynn loved her career, but never more than she loved us. She'd already proven that by canceling on several events or refusing contracts that conflicted with the boys' sports schedules or when one of them was the same night as Dylan's school Christmas pageant.

Brynn was a more incredible mother than I'd even imagined when we'd been in this cabin for the first time eleven years ago. And that was nothing on how she was as a wife. Every day I woke up and felt like the luckiest man alive. She was the best partner in life I could've ever asked for.

She caught me staring at her and her smile grew. "What are you doing all the way up there? All the fun's down here."

"I'm coming down now," I hollered back.

I ripped off my shirt, since I was already wearing my swim trunks, and even from this distance I could see the way her eyes heated at the sight. I wasn't as ripped as I'd been when we got married, but she assured me all the time that she found my dad bod droolworthy. As long as she liked it, I was happy.

I grabbed the two-person kayak on my way to the dock. "Hey bud, wanna go out on the water while Mom and Adam do swim lessons?" I asked Dylan.

His little face lit up. "Yeah!"

These were the moments I lived for—enjoying life with my family and building memories we'd all carry for the rest of our lives.

I pulled off my reading glasses and set them down on the nightstand along with my phone. At the same time, Brynn walked out of the bathroom, rubbing lotion on her hands.

"What's that grin for?" she asked.

"Sully ordered another table. I swear he's going to single-handedly keep me in business."

I'd started a woodworking business like she'd suggested. Sometimes it was small things, but mostly it was big wooden pieces of furniture. It had been more fulfilling than I'd expected.

She came over to the bed and straddled my waist. She was wearing one of my T-shirts, and when I slid my hands up her thighs, I discovered she was completely naked underneath. Wrapping her arms around my neck, she ground that pussy I was addicted to along my boxer briefs where my cock was already growing hard. "Sounds like we should celebrate."

I nuzzled her neck. "I don't need a reason to fuck you, but if you want to call it celebrating, then sure."

She chuckled and then gripped my head with her hands, pushing me back so she could look in my eyes. "I'm proud of you, ya know."

If it was possible for a heart to melt, mine would've in that moment. "Thanks baby. I couldn't do any of this without you. I wouldn't want to."

"Me either," she said right before she closed the distance between us and kissed me. It was soft and slow, the kind of kiss that came with the security of knowing you were kissing your person. There was no rush because we knew we had time.

Certainly more time than we'd had when the boys were little. They slept harder now that they were eight and six, which meant there was less chance of us getting interrupted.

She rolled her hips, rubbing her slick pussy over me. "You better help me get these off so I can feel that pretty pussy sliding on my bare cock," I said, referring to my boxer briefs.

She moaned into my mouth as our kiss grew deeper, needier. I moved my hands from where they were on her thighs and gently pushed her back enough so that I could finagle my underwear off. She helped pull it off the rest of my legs and my feet and then settled back right where she belonged.

"Fuck, you always feel so fucking good," I murmured against her lush pink lips before I sealed my mouth over hers and plundered her mouth with my tongue. She melted against me while her hips rocked back and forth at a quicker pace.

"You gonna come on my cock like this, baby?"

"No. You're gonna stick that big dick inside and stretch me out." She leaned to the side, whispering against my ear. "And then I'm going to come on that cock."

Fuck, I loved it when she talked dirty.

With a groan, I brought her mouth back to mine and kissed her hard. At the same time, she slid her hand between us, gripping my cock at its base and then notching it against her wet heat. With teasing slowness, she eased down on my cock, both of us moaning as her pussy stretched around my girth.

"Oh fuck, Wy."

I needed her naked. I slipped my hands under the hem of the T-shirt and pulled it up her body. Once I tossed it to the side, I nipped at her collarbone. "Ride me until you come."

I moved my mouth down her chest to her perfect tits. She was worried they were sagging more since she'd had the boys, but I didn't care if they sagged to her belly button—they didn't, but I wouldn't have cared anyway—they were still perfect to me.

She rocked faster, rubbing her clit against my lower abs, her fingers sliding into my hair that I'd grown out a bit so she had something more to hold on to during moments like this.

Her breathing grew more labored. "Oh...G-God," she whimpered, her hips stuttering as she teetered on the edge. But I wasn't about to have her stop now, not when I was craving the feel of her pussy squeezing my dick so hard I'd see stars.

Gripping her hips, I moved her back and forth over my body, picking up the pace that she couldn't carry anymore on her own. Her thighs started to tremble and then she buried her face in my neck and let out a low, stifled moan as her pussy choked my cock with her orgasm. My eyes closed in bliss at the sensation and then I was bucking into her recklessly until my own orgasm hit me like a truck.

Her body remained limp against me as we both caught our breath. "Fuck, you always feel so good."

She sat up, her delicate hands cupping my neck. "Even after eleven years together?"

I sat up taller, pulling her tight to my chest. "Brynn, you would still feel good after an eternity together. You were made for me."

Resting her forehead against mine, she whispered, "I love you, Wyatt."

"I love you too, baby. Never doubt that."

"I don't."

"Good. Because you're my heart, my life. I'm nothing without you." She knew this, but I still told her often.

"Same for me."

I kissed her again, soft and slow, and then lay down, keeping her body draped across the top of me, my dick softening but still inside her. We'd need to clean up before we went to bed, but right now I just wanted to soak up this quiet moment of happiness with my wife.

We would continue to experience highs and lows in the future, just like we had in the past, but I knew without a single doubt that we'd always have each other.

And that was all that mattered.

AFTERWORD

I originally thought this was going to be Grant and Shannon's story, but they decided to stop talking to me while Wyatt couldn't stop. As soon as I stopped fighting it, the words flew onto the page. I've loved Wyatt since his appearance in Only a Kiss and I'm so excited he finally gets his own happily ever after.

This book wouldn't be possible without the help of some incredible people I'm blessed to have in my life.

A huge thank you to my editors, Happily Editing Anns. You are a critical part of my team and I value you and your feedback so much.

Thank you to my amazingly talented friend at Lily Bear Design Co who designed the discreet covers for this series.

To my beta readers Kelly and Alyse. Thank you for your feedback so I could really make this story sparkle :)

To the Sleuth Squad (you know who you are), thank you for keeping me sane and cheering me on when I get discouraged. I love you ladies!

As always, to my incredible husband for taking care of the kids so mommy could hide away and write for a little while. And for always making sure I'm drinking enough water.

To my miracle babies, for giving me the motivation to chase my dreams. I love you both so much.

And last, but never least, to you the reader. Whether you just found my books or have been reading them since the beginning, I couldn't do this without you. Thank you!

ABOUT THE AUTHOR

Cadence Keys is a bestselling steamy romance author. When she's not coming up with plots for her books, she's chasing her rambunctious toddlers around or cuddling with her husband. She loves writing heartfelt stories with relatable characters and a guaranteed happily ever after.

Learn more about her and her books on her website: www.cadencekeysauthor.com

facebook.com/cadencekeysauthor

x.com/cadencewrites

instagram.com/cadencekeysauthor

bookbub.com/profile/cadence-keys

goodreads.com/cadencekeysauthor

tiktok.com/@cadencekeysauthor

ALSO BY CADENCE KEYS

LA Wolves Football Series

In the Grasp

Across the Middle

Down by Contact

Taking the Handoff

Scorched Turf (Author Website Exclusive Novella)

Defending the Backfield

After the Snap

Closing the Distance

Protecting the Boundary

Rapturous Intent Rockstar Series

Noble Intent

Forbidden Intent

Devoted Intent

Promised Intent

Breaking the Rules Series

Only a Kiss

Just for Tonight

About Last Night